THE BET

"Well, in my books," Sally sputtered, "Clemmie's just a plain, ordinary old bore, and nothing's ever going to change that."

"I don't agree with that," said Felicity. "I read in the *Family Guide* that any girl can be made to stand out in a crowd. With a little work, Clemmie could sparkle."

Jane and Sally simultaneously burst out laughing.

"Clemmie sparkle?" Jane cackled. "It would take the entire Milky Way to make her shine!"

"I don't think so. A change of hairstyle, perhaps, and a new costume . . . I could make Clemmie one of the most popular girls in Avonlea."

Even for Felicity, this was a pretty rash claim. Sally's eyes opened up very wide.

"Don't give yourself airs, Felicity King."

Instantly, without even thinking about what she was getting into, Felicity responded to the challenge.

"I'll bet I can."

Also available in the Road to Avonlea series from Bantam Skylark Books

Felicity's Challenge

Storybook written by
Gail Hamilton

Based on the Sullivan Films Production
written by Lori Fleming
adapted from the novels of

Lucy Maud Montgomery

A BANTAM SKYLARK BOOK
NEW YORK • TORONTO • LONDON • SYDNEY • AUCKLAND

*Based on the Sullivan Films Production produced by Sullivan Films Inc.
in association with CBC and the Disney Channel with the participation of
Telefilm Canada adapted from Lucy Maud Montgomery's novels.*

*Teleplay written by Lori Fleming
Copyright © 1989 by Sullivan Films Distribution, Inc.*

*This edition contains the complete text
of the original edition.*
NOT ONE WORD HAS BEEN OMITTED.

RL 6, 008–012

FELICITY'S CHALLENGE

*A Bantam Skylark Book / published by arrangement with
HarperCollins Publishers Ltd.*

PRINTING HISTORY

*HarperCollins edition published 1991
Bantam edition / December 1992*

ROAD TO AVONLEA is the trademark of Sullivan Films Inc.

*Skylark Books is a registered trademark of Bantam Books,
a division of Bantam Doubleday Dell Publishing Group, Inc.
Registered in U.S. Patent and Trademark Office and elsewhere.*

Chapter One

Saturday afternoon was the busiest time of the week in Avonlea. Most of the people thereabouts took the opportunity to get dressed up, do their shopping and have a fine old visit with the friends and neighbors they met at every corner. So naturally, Saturday was the day any shrewd politician would pick to stir up support for himself. Election time was fast coming up on Prince Edward Island.

Judson Parker was just such an enterprising fellow. He had tossed his hat into the political ring with a flourish and was determined to get his hands on the local seat. Consequently, he was working Avonlea's main street with so much energy and bluster that he could practically be heard through the walls of every house in the village.

Judson was a ruddy, corpulent man with an overfed look, an overpowering laugh and eyes that shifted around too much to vouch for absolute probity of character. On top of this, he had dressed himself in a loud checked suit and an even louder striped cravat in order to make himself look desirable to the Avonlea citizens. To gain the seat, Judson would have to defeat the incumbent, one David Amsberry, who had been serving the area quite to its satisfaction for the last ten years. Anxious on this account, Judson saw every man, woman and child in Avonlea as the one who could make the difference between winning and losing the election.

Judson worked in concert with his sidekick and constant companion, Herschel. Herschel was a born follower. Thin, owl-eyed and obsequious, Herschel trotted at Judson's heels like a faithful pup, carrying Judson's campaign pamphlets, reminding Judson of details too petty for the great man to remember himself and constantly agreeing with everything Judson said. Herschel was the perfect choice for an aide-de-camp. Compared to Herschel, even a fence post would look as though it had leadership potential.

Judson had done his homework about Avonlea and had mapped out a campaign strategy. Ever on the watch for the right persons to impress, Judson dodged nimbly around a passing hay wagon to intercept none other than Mrs. Potts, president of the Women's Improvement Society and the biggest gossip for miles around. Mrs. Potts considered herself someone to be reckoned with in Avonlea affairs, and beamed with pleasure that Judson had recognized her importance. Judson doffed his hat and, at the same time, indicated the busy scene around them with a sweep of his arm.

"Avonlea is very fortunate to be such a prosperous little community," Judson rumbled. "The beauty of the village is a credit to its Improvement Society and is matched by the loveliness of Avonlea's ladies themselves, Mrs. Potts."

Judson was as happy to lay on the flattery as Mrs. Potts was to lap it up. Though far from picturesque, Mrs. Potts adorned her person with as many buttons, feathers and bows as she could manage, and she imagined herself one of the chief ornaments of the neighborhood. Her eyelashes fluttered quite ridiculously at Judson and Herschel.

"Well, gentlemen, we ladies do our best to enhance the appearance of our village."

"And how much it's appreciated by the Islanders." With a hand laid feelingly to his bosom, Judson favored Mrs. Potts with such a deferential bow that the lady would have giggled aloud had she thought she could get away with it.

Seeing Mrs. Potts nicely softened up, Judson smiled, showing his large yellow teeth, and got straight to his real purpose.

"If you would do me the honor to give me your support in the election next week, I will make a firm promise to support any endeavors you may institute to beautify this town."

"And he's a man of his word," Herschel added, bobbing up and down like a cork in a bucket of water.

Mrs. Potts swelled visibly with gratification and patted at her hair. She was not known for her ability to see through windy promises and slick remarks.

"Oh, well, you can count on my support, Mr. Parker, and you can be sure I'll pass on your remarks to the other members of the Avonlea

Improvement Society, who I'm certain will follow suit."

Judson's smile widened. "Oh, a charming pleasure, to be sure, Mrs. Potts. Give her some brochures, Herschel."

Obediently, Herschel reached into his satchel and produced a handful of Parker campaign literature. Judson took the pamphlets and held them out to Mrs. Potts.

"Perhaps you will accept some of these brochures. You might care to distribute them to some of your select friends."

Of course, Judson's manner implied, a woman of Mrs. Potts's refinement would have only select friends and certainly no ordinary ones. Hook, line and sinker, Mrs. Potts swallowed the bait.

"The pleasure is all mine, and I'll be sure my husband reads it thoroughly as well. After all," Mrs. Potts cooed, "he's the one doing the voting."

In Prince Edward Island, only the men could vote. Now and then in Charlottetown there were demonstrations by suffragettes, and then, even in Avonlea, there would be talk of giving women the vote. Men scoffed heartily at the idea, politicians blanched and few people believed such a fantastic notion would ever become a reality. However, no political campaigner ever underestimated the influence a strong-minded woman had over her husband.

Mrs. Potts chuckled at her own humorous sally. Judson, hastily seconded by Herschel, joined in, though he did sound a little contrived about it. A man seeking political favor must learn to laugh at any kind of joke by any kind of joker, even a leading member of the Avonlea Improvement Society.

Clutching her brochures, Mrs. Potts moved off, leaving Judson to peer about for his next victim. The wide berth he had on the otherwise busy street might have discouraged him had he not noticed a knot of curious people gathering around a large poster reading "Farmers! Vote for Judson Parker!" In a wink, Judson had thrust himself, large as life, in front of his own portrait on the poster.

"Let me introduce myself," he boomed out in his speechifying voice. "I am Judson Parker, your candidate for Member of the Legislative Assembly."

The group transferred its attentions to Judson but didn't exhibit much enthusiasm. In fact, as soon as Judson showed signs of breaking into a speech, people swiftly remembered where it was they had been going and hurried away. Judson found himself striking an oratorical pose in front of two startled horses and a patch of trodden mud.

Swiveling his head, Judson then spotted a thirteen-year-old girl coming towards him carrying a basket. Though she looked like about the last person to have political influence, Judson brightened at once and stepped in front of her.

"Oh, miss, excuse me."

Felicity King halted in surprise. Large politicians were not in the habit of addressing her.

"You're Alec King's daughter, aren't you?"

The Kings were about the most prosperous and respected family in the district, and Judson was ready to use any method to get to them, even buttonholing the children.

"Yes, I am." Felicity smiled politely.

At once, Judson whipped out a fistful of brochures.

"I meant to give your father these. Would you be good enough to pass them along? Tell him I will drop in as I promised, as soon as he's had a chance to look at them." Parker paused for effect, as he mentally reached into his bag of tricks. "I, uh, want to make a donation."

"As a prize," Herschel prompted speedily, knowing just where the prize stood on the list of items Judson was prepared to give out in order to rake in votes.

"As a prize," Judson continued. "Yes, for this year's Harvest Celebration Party."

If Judson wanted Felicity's interest, he certainly had it now. The Harvest Party was one of the biggest Avonlea events of the year and one where Felicity always shone. At the mention of a prize, Felicity became more than merely polite. Her eyes lit up and her head filled with all sorts of interesting possibilities. After all, prizes were meant to be won and someone had to win them. Someone who might very well be herself. She took the brochures obligingly.

"Yes," she assured Judson, "I'll be sure to tell him."

"Yes, do," Judson murmured under his breath as he watched Felicity trot happily off. If he could get a King vote in the bag, the rest of Avonlea would likely follow suit.

Chapter Two

In Avonlea, the general store served not only as a place to buy things, but also as a handy social center where people lingered to exchange the news. The store was a cluttered, comfortable place with a big wooden counter and rows of shelves crammed with every conceivable thing that Avonlea and the farms surrounding it might need. Bolts of fabric, ladies' hats, bottles of horse liniment, overalls, teeth for mowers, boxes of baking powder, nails and sealing rings crowded each other for space. The smell of spices and harness leather and squeaky newness filled the lungs agreeably as soon as the door swung open.

Today, three Avonlea farmers—Amos Spry, Harmon Andrews and Alec King—stood by the window looking out over the flour bags at Judson and Herschel. Mrs. Lawson, who owned the store with her husband, worked behind the counter unpacking glass lamp globes that had just been delivered that morning by the freight wagon from the railway station.

"Just look at that Judson Parker," said Amos Spry, sticking his thumbs into his suspenders. "First time he's run for office, acting like he's been in politics for years."

Avonlea people didn't like upstarts thrust upon them. They preferred a man to work his way up in the community before aspiring to represent them in the Legislature. That way, they at least knew what sort of bargain they were getting.

"Well, he has been in politics a while," put in Harmon Andrews with a wink, "but not up front. And nothing's been proved, mind you, but...well, put it this way—he's got a shady reputation."

Amos nodded knowingly, as though he had firm suspicions of every shady deal for miles around.

"Well, rumor goes that he's got his finger in every political pie that's cooked."

"Mmm, some people say all his fingers," quipped Alec King with a grin.

"Oh, Alec!" Mrs. Lawson chided, even as she burst out laughing with Amos and Harmon.

At that moment, Felicity entered the store, carrying her collection of campaign literature, her eyes still bright at the thought of a prize.

"Ah, there's my girl."

Alec King smiled at the sight of his eldest daughter, rosy-cheeked from the crisp fall air. Felicity was a very tidy, handsome girl who took a good deal of pride in her appearance. With her perky tam and her scarf flung over one shoulder, she looked quite the little lady.

"Hello, Father."

With great ceremony, Felicity handed the brochures to him.

"Mr. Parker asked me to give these to you. He

said something about a prize for this year's Harvest Party," she added hopefully.

In spite of Felicity's eagerness, Alec King frowned and rubbed his chin.

"Hmm, likely a prize for himself for prompting the most number of women to sway their husbands' votes."

Clearly, Alec had a lot more respect for the direct approach than for a sly attempt to gain influence through the female side of Avonlea.

Seeing that the men were going to start talking politics again, Mrs. Lawson put the last of the lamp globes on the shelf behind her and came out from behind the counter.

"Felicity, I have that piece of leftover fabric I promised you."

Forgetting all about Judson Parker for the moment, Felicity followed Mrs. Lawson into the back room in search of the cloth. Felicity loved to sew and was always making pretty things for herself. Mrs. Lawson knew just what to save for Felicity.

Back by the window, Amos Spry shook his head at Judson's campaign literature. Amos didn't believe a word printed on it and said so unequivocally.

"Well, it's six of one, half dozen of the other if

you ask me. Politicians are all alike, promising the moon, but it all goes by the wayside after they're elected."

"Well, I can't agree with you there," Alec commented, tossing the brochures aside. "I mean, David Amsberry has represented this area for a long time. He's done a good job. He's got my vote again."

"Mine too," said Harmon Andrews, turning his back on the window to examine some tools. "That's one heck of a price to pay for a rake," he exclaimed, holding one up for inspection.

Amos Spry grinned at Alec. Harmon was known to be mighty tight with a dollar.

"That's a heck of a rake."

Outside, Judson was still concentrating on the women and children of Avonlea. He had cornered a mother and her little boy who had been trying to ease their way quietly past the poster, their minds on other things. Judson, who was a veritable cornucopia of bribes, pulled a fistful of candies from his pocket and thrust them at the child. Then Judson laughed as the boy, unable to believe his luck, began stuffing them, as fast as he could, into his mouth. The boy was not allowed to eat candies and knew that his mother would confiscate the loot the minute the noisy man went away.

"Now don't you eat all those toffees at once," chuckled Judson as he straightened to speak to the mother. "And you make sure you let your husband have a look at those brochures we gave you, madam."

The woman was more intent on getting her child away from Judson's influence than anything else. Stuffing the brochures into her shopping bag, she nodded just to escape. Luckily for her, Amos Spry stepped out of the general store at just that moment, heading for his wagon. Judson was immediately at his side.

"Good day to you, Mr. Spry," Judson greeted him jovially, falling in step with the farmer.

"And to you, sir."

Though surprised that Judson even knew his name, Amos gave a tip of his hat and tried to continue on his way. Before he reached his wagon, however, Judson was on his heels. Even fat politicians can be very fast on their feet when they have their own advantage in view.

"How's the family?" Judson inquired, speaking as though the condition of the Sprys had been the most pressing thing on his mind all day. "You have a new addition, I hear."

Amos was even more surprised. The Sprys hadn't even got round to putting a birth announcement in the paper. Birth announcements cost money, and a new Spry was no longer much of a novelty in Avonlea.

"We do, at that," he admitted, hefting his few purchases into the back of his wagon.

"Well now, my, my, that makes it—what—" Judson peered into the atmosphere to solicit a number, "seven now, doesn't it?"

Thinking of his ever-expanding family, Amos sighed. "Yes, it's a bit of a handful at times."

When Amos went to untie his team, he found Judson between himself and the hitching post.

"And how's the harvest? It's not a very good year for potatoes."

Faced with Judson's persistence, Amos paused a minute to lay a work-hardened hand on the neck of his horse.

"Well, you're right there," he admitted slowly. "Half of them are runts, the other half green and sproutin'."

Potatoes were Prince Edward Island's main crop, and a long-suffering vegetable they were, too. However, even potatoes had their limits. If the weather got too wet or too cold, potatoes refused to grow big enough to be useful. If the soil got washed from their tops, they turned an inedible green and sprouted spongily from their eyes. Since there was no market for potatoes like that, an unlucky farmer could find himself with seven sprouting children and hardly any income for the year.

Judson seemed to know Amos's situation perfectly. He patted the protruding bulk of his stomach and looked grave.

"Yes, the, uh...ahem, manager at the bank in Summerside is a little, ah, concerned, shall we say, whether you're able to repay your loan on time. He and I are very good friends," he added, conspiratorially.

Amos Spry's mouth fell open. What good was taking his money troubles into a bank manager's private office if the whole countryside was going to know about them before the week was out. Instantly, Amos was bristling all over.

"What business is it of yours or his to be discussing my affairs?"

This angry outburst failed to offend Judson at all. In fact, he laid his hand on Amos's shoulder in a brotherly fashion and looked more concerned than ever.

"Oh, come now, my good man. It's my business if I'm able to offer you a little, um, help."

"Like what, Mr. Parker?" Amos demanded suspiciously. He had got his horses untied at last and intended to drive off smartly as soon as he was able. If there was anything that irked a Prince Edward Island farmer, it was the idea that somebody else was privy to his financial woes.

Casually, Judson laid his hand on the bridle of the bay mare next to him. She jerked her head in annoyance but could not get away. With one heel, Judson kicked idly at the dust near her hooves.

"Well, I might be able to, uh, talk about the, uh, loan terms—ask the bank to, um, ease up."

"To relax," Herschel supplied, popping out from his regular place just behind Judson. He had been hovering in the background, so much like a gangling shadow that Amos had scarcely noticed him. Just as Amos was about to grow doubly affronted at having Judson's underling in on his problems too, Judson clapped him soundly on the back.

"I'm very proud of the honest farmer," he declared expansively, "backbone of the economy. Besides, I, uh, I'd be a whole lot more lenient than a bank if I were to lend you the money myself."

"That's true," Herschel said, emphasizing with a gulp of his Adam's apple just how proud Judson could be.

"Especially if you were able to, uh, scratch my back as well..."

Judson winked in a confidential sort of way. The wink got Judson's meaning across without Judson actually having to come out and say that the price of the loan would be Amos's vote.

By now, Amos had stopped trying to climb up into his wagon and stood still, uncertainly. He did have seven children to feed and they were all getting touchy about eating potatoes. The bank had him in a corner and he couldn't deny it. He didn't much like Judson Parker, but the man was dangling a mighty powerful temptation in front of him.

"Well," he conceded, not looking at either Judson or Herschel, "I'd be willing to listen, Parker. I mean, um," he had to swallow hard to get the last part out, "maybe it is time for a change."

"Yes, for a change," Herschel chimed in.

"Yes, indeed." Judson stepped back then so that Amos could finally hoist himself up into the wagon. Shrewdly, Judson said no more about the offer, but his slight smile as Amos turned his team into the street indicated that he thought the bargain sealed and the Spry vote assured.

Chapter Three

"Oww!" Felicity squawked, clapping her hand to her mouth to muffle the sound. Getting caught making indignant noises was a serious matter in the Avonlea school, even if a person like Felicity had just been snapped in a tender part of her anatomy by an expertly aimed rubber band.

Felicity could only glare at the perpetrator, Edward Ray, who sat behind her, grinning at his prank. Edward was a lanky, energetic boy of about Felicity's age who loved to get Felicity's attention any way he could. Since his methods bordered on the outrageous, he often drove Felicity into a seething fury.

Felicity had to seethe in silence. Though her own aunt, Hetty King, was the schoolmistress, it was no advantage to be a relative. Stiff penalties were in order for anyone caught disturbing the peace.

Hetty was, at that moment, writing on the blackboard and rapidly losing her patience with all the restless shifting among the children at their desks behind her. The last hour of the last day of the school week tended to make the children regard their seats the same way frogs regard hot griddles. All they wanted to do was spring up from them and dash away into the freedom waiting just outside.

Finishing at the blackboard, she turned around. The eldest of the King family, Hetty was a tall, angular woman who ran the school along strict principles.

"'Harvest Time,'" she began, turning a gimlet eye upon the children. "Though the weather's certainly taken a nasty turn, 'Harvest Time' is our recitation topic for the month. You've all had ample time to prepare."

This announcement was greeted by unenthusiastic groans. Even Sara Stanley, who was brilliant at recitations, could not prevent herself from fiddling with her inkwell and gazing out the window. Twelve-year-old Sara was Felicity's cousin. Besides having Hetty King as a teacher and an aunt, Sara lived with her as well. This made misbehaving in the classroom doubly perilous, and Sara had no intention of jeopardizing her liberty this late in the day.

Felicity's younger brother, eleven-year-old Felix, peeped enviously at Edward's small collection of rubber bands while Clemmie Ray, Edward's little sister, lost her nerve about passing a note to Cecily King, her best friend and the youngest of the King children.

Further back, Sally Potts and Jane Spry dared whisper to each other. Sally and Jane sat together at a double desk as far away from Miss King as they could. It was a case of birds of a feather flocking together—nasty birds, in this case, for Sally and Jane were natural troublemakers. They couldn't help stirring up mischief whenever they got the chance and then gloating over the results. The grimace Jane made about the recitation topic caused several children around her to snicker behind their hands. Hetty rapped her pointer sharply on her desk.

"I'm well aware that this is Friday afternoon and that all you have in your heads is the Harvest Party tomorrow evening, but may I remind you that we still have half an hour before school is dismissed, and I intend to make the most of it. Is that clear?"

The grins vanished and the children hastily dragged their attention back from the windows. They could all see that Miss Hetty King was reaching her limit.

"Yes, Miss King," the class replied, hoping to get through the last segment of the day without running afoul of Hetty's temper. Hetty was capable of keeping the entire room in after school if they provoked her enough.

"Good," she replied, pleased with the effect she had on potential wrongdoers. "Now that you're all properly settled, we shall proceed with the recitation assignments. Let me see..."

With a jolt, the class realized that Hetty was going to make them start on the Harvest Time recitations then and there, when they had all counted on escaping this ordeal until at least the following Monday. Only one pupil dared raise her hand. The rest slowly sank down in their desks like chickens trying to make themselves invisible when the hawk flies over, doing their best to avoid Hetty's eye. As with the chickens, there had to be a victim. Hetty caught sight of a ducking head and swung her pointer to the side of the room.

"Clemmie Ray, what have you prepared to tell the class?"

Clemmie turned instantly pale at being singled out. A plain, plump child, eleven-year-old Clemmie was not blessed with a great many social graces. On top of all this, Clemmie's biggest terror on earth was of having to stand up and give a speech. She had put off her preparations until after the Harvest Party, hoping not to even have to think about public speaking until the weekend had passed. Now she was caught cold with no speech composed and no courage in her breast to confess the fact.

Hetty walked to the back of the classroom, turned around and stood there expectantly. Clemmie saw there was nothing for it but to stand up and give the speech a try. Quaking like a prisoner led to the gallows, she slowly rose from her desk and made her way to a spot just in front of the blackboard.

"Harvest Time," she whispered hoarsely by way of introduction.

Even if she had prepared a speech, it wouldn't have done any good. Every word would have flown out of Clemmie's mind, leaving it as blank and echoing as it was at that very moment. The rows of watching faces turned her innards to jelly and her voice to a thread. Clemmie simply stood there. Except for her wringing hands, she was petrified.

"You may begin, Clemmie," Hetty prompted.

Clemmie remained speechless, her eyes growing bigger and her face turning chalkier. Though she had known nearly everyone in the class all her life, they might as well have been transformed into a horde of drooling cannibals bent on gobbling her up alive.

"Oh, come now, child," cajoled Hetty, unable

to see the room from Clemmie's perspective. "You're among friends."

This wasn't strictly true. Sally Potts and Jane Spry snickered together at Clemmie's predicament. Neither of them liked Clemmie and they were tickled to see her put in such an uncomfortable spot. Hetty quelled them with a sideways glance.

"And we're all very interested to hear what you have to say, *aren't* we, class?"

"Yes, Miss King," the class dutifully replied, without the least regard for the truth. The last thing they wanted so close to dismissal time was a bumbling recitation about pumpkins and sheaves of wheat.

Clemmie gulped a tremendous breath.

"Harvest Time," she began again, heroically screwing herself up to the ordeal before her. "Well, Harvest Time is my most favorite time of year."

This seemed a safe enough statement. Since the floor didn't swallow her up or the roof tremble, Clemmie felt heartened. Drawing in a second, shaky breath, she cast frantically around in her mind for something else to add.

"That is because it is when people get together and do things to get ready for winter—picking apples, baking. I..."

Clemmie faltered suddenly. Jane Spry had just held up her slate in such a way that only Clemmie could see it. On the slate, Jane had drawn the picture of a pig. Jane, not being much of an artist, had drawn the pig cross-eyed, lop-sided and very ugly. Underneath the pig, Jane had written, "Clemmie."

"I—I like the smell outside," Clemmie squeezed out, "and...and I loved the smell inside of pies—"

Making sure she was out of Hetty's sight, Jane pushed up the end of her nose and silently imitated the grunting of a pig. Desperately, Clemmie clung to her rapidly fraying shred of thought.

"Pies—pies—pies and preserves."

Her throat closed up and a horrible silence ensued, a silence filled with the rustle of young bodies twisting in their seats, coughs and smoth-ered mirth. In agony, Clemmie groped for one more fact, any fact, about the harvest.

"Please continue, Clemmie," Hetty said, lest Clemmie be imagining her speech was over.

Jane, still unseen by Hetty, continued to flash the pig picture and make grunting motions. She was quickly joined by Sally Potts, who did an even better pig imitation than Jane. Sally was helped in this by having a broad nose, goggly eyes and a naturally porcine expression.

Sara Stanley caught a sudden glimpse of their games and looked disgusted. Sara knew all about the hazards of public speaking. She had been rooting for Clemmie and hated to see her crashing down in ignominious ruin. Yet Sara could do absolutely nothing to help Clemmie, who was now turning a violent beet color and twisting distractedly at her cuff. Even Hetty could see that Clemmie had done all the public speaking she was capable of that day. She waved one hand dismissively.

"Goodness! Well, never mind. Take your seat. You'll simply have to try it again next week."

"Yes, Miss King."

Still a blotchy scarlet, Clemmie fled in disgrace back to her desk where she put her head down, refusing to look at anybody. Clemmie was the sort of child who felt her failure acutely, and she would suffer from this one the whole weekend through.

As Hetty turned around, Felicity was caught with her head bent close to Sara's, completely unaware that Hetty's gaze had settled upon her.

"It's going to be the longest train of satin that you've ever seen," Felicity was whispering. "Much longer than my princess costume from last year."

Caught up in describing her costume for the annual Harvest Party, Felicity completely forgot about the larger dangers to which she was exposing herself. Hetty descended upon her directly.

"Felicity King! Well, since you evidently don't have any trouble talking, perhaps you'd like to favor us with your recitation."

A less composed person might have been flung by this order into total disarray. Not Felicity. Unlike a good many others, she took pride in doing her work on time, and very often far in advance. Confidently, she rose and took her place at the blackboard, her hands neatly folded in front of her.

"Harvest Time," she began smoothly. "Harvest time is the most wonderful time of the year. It is the time when we celebrate the bounty of the harvest, which we always conclude with a Harvest Party."

Thoughts of the long satin train made Felicity look very pleased with herself for a moment. Sally and Jane, disliking Felicity even more than Clemmie, yawned in elaborate boredom. Edward Ray, though, found himself directly in Felicity's line of vision and didn't hesitate to make use of his luck. Immediately, he began to cross his eyes and make comical faces, all the while keeping his head so still that Hetty, behind him, never guessed what dastardly tricks he was really up to.

Ignoring him, Felicity continued with her speech, self-righteous and sure of herself.

"Many hands make light work," Felicity announced, looking as proud as though she had just made that up herself. "And at Harvest Time, it is especially important to join together with all of our friends to help each other out. I consider myself very lucky to have many friends."

Sometimes Felicity was altogether too conscious of her own virtue. Today was one of those times. She couldn't help but sound as though she put friends in the same category as long satin trains or plenty of jam in the cupboard.

Sara rolled her eyes ceilingward. She was Felicity's friend, but that didn't stop her from admitting that Felicity could be a pain sometimes. Edward sucked in his cheeks, stuck out his front teeth and wriggled his ears, an accomplishment Felicity was finding harder and harder not to stare at. She lifted her chin and fixed her eyes squarely on Queen Victoria's picture on the wall at the back.

"You can measure the worth of a person by the number of friends he or she possesses. In life, things may come..."

Edward made his scalp twitch at the front. His nose seemed to pull to one side and his tongue curled so far down over his lower lip it looked as though it might come right out at the root. Unable to stop herself, Felicity glanced away from the Queen's portrait. Edward's atrocious faces finally succeeded in making her stumble.

"And...things may go, but we always have our friends. I think that...that...*Edward!*"

Edward's name just exploded from Felicity. She snapped her mouth shut and glared at her tormentor, furious that he had managed to derail her speech and prod her into an outburst. Now she would probably lose marks for presentation, all because Edward was such a perverse, insufferable, maddening boy. Edward shook with silent, gleeful laughter. Hetty pressed her lips into a thin, ominous line.

"That's enough, Felicity. Take your seat."

Sally and Jane, overjoyed by Felicity's downfall, could hardly hide their supercilious smirks. Edward looked pleased enough to burst, for now Felicity was sure to be thinking about him for days. Livid with suppressed outrage, Felicity reached over as she walked to her desk and pinched Edward as hard as she could.

"Oww!" he croaked, astonished that Felicity,

victim of so many rubber bands, should so suddenly and unexpectedly retaliate. But even Felicity, who cared so much about decorum, had her limits.

Hetty might have missed the faces and the giggles, but she could hardly miss this. It was the last straw.

"Felicity King, that was inexcusable. My class is not a three-ring circus. Nor do we take public speaking lightly here."

Hetty marched to the front of the room, swinging her pointer meaningfully.

"In years to come, you'll be expected to discourse in front of audiences far more critical than one made up of your own peers. I have no patience with pupils who take so little pride in their presentations."

Felicity's nostrils flared. She had been taking her presentation quite seriously indeed—if only she had been allowed to keep on with it. Her only satisfaction was in the fierceness with which she had pinched Edward.

Hetty was on the verge of a further lecture, but a glance at the clock informed her that she would be doing it after school hours. She set down her pointer. Teachers like to get home after school just as much as anyone else.

"Well, we'll stop for the day, as it's almost three. However, because of that display of hooliganism, Felicity, you'll stay behind and help this week's cleaning team. I'm sure that Clemmie and Sara will be grateful for your assistance."

Provoked by this gross injustice, Felicity looked as though she were on the verge of a mutinous explosion. However, she knew better than to challenge her Aunt Hetty. She actually had to bite her lower lip to repress an angry retort as Sally and Jane laughed behind her and Sally stuck out her tongue. This time, Hetty spotted the miscreants.

"Jane Spry, Sally Potts, as you seem to find this carnival atmosphere so appealing, you can stay behind and help as well."

Ah, retribution! Felicity smirked outright and, taking care that Hetty didn't see, stuck out her tongue at Sally in return.

"The rest of the class is dismissed," Hetty announced. At the first word, the children flew out of their seats and started racing out the door. Hetty put on her own hat and coat.

"Sara, mind you don't dally behind with the others. I want you home before dark," Hetty ordered. Then she turned to the rest of the unfortunates who were left behind. "Well, now, I expect to find a perfect job done when I come in here on Monday morning. Good afternoon, girls."

Five faces turned to her dolefully.

"Good afternoon, Miss King."

Chapter Four

The minute Hetty was out the door, Felicity whirled on Edward Ray, who had contrived to dawdle behind.

"Edward Ray, you are dreadful beyond words!"

Infuriatingly, Edward grinned back at her. He was still fingering one of the offending rubber bands.

"All the girls who've ever liked me always say the same."

Felicity's mouth popped open.

"Like you? I can't stand you!"

Still grinning, Edward wriggled his ears again, as though the very vehemence of Felicity's words were proof of her fascination with him. Slowly, teasingly, he backed towards the door, keeping a vigilant eye on Felicity in case of retaliatory action. Sara, who had seen Edward during Felicity's speech, came to her cousin's defense.

"Ignore him, Felicity. Like a bad cold, he's bound to go away sooner or later."

Turning on her heel, Felicity got a damp cloth and began to wipe off the blackboard. The rest of the girls, following suit, got busy too. They all wanted to get on their way home as soon as possible, but they knew they'd end up staying late again next week if the classroom was not tidied up to Hetty's satisfaction. Sally and Jane took out brooms from the broom closet and started sweeping the floor while Sara dusted the desks. Clemmie, still shaken from the fiery ruin of her speech, lifted the chalky erasers from their ledge.

"Honestly, Clemmie," Felicity burst out, "I don't know what's got into your brother lately, but he certainly is a pest."

Felicity absolutely hated public humiliation. Though Edward had finally left, she couldn't get her persecutor out of her head.

"He still likes you, you know, Felicity," Sara commented, going over the desks as rapidly as she could.

Felicity huffed in disgust at such a ridiculous idea.

Sally smirked from behind her broom. "Oh, Felicity," she cooed, "he's stuck on you like a fly on molasses."

"All I know is," Felicity muttered, "the next time I have to get up in front of the class, I'll take a sack, put it over his head and tie it up at the neck."

Everyone giggled at this idea, except Clemmie, who was beyond giggling for the moment. She started pounding the erasers together with all her might. A great cloud of chalk dust mushroomed around her, making Sally Potts sneeze.

"Clemmie, don't do that in here! You're getting it all over the floor." And what was on the floor Sally would have to sweep up.

"Oh, sorry," Clemmie apologized hastily from amidst the cloud. Some days, Clemmie felt, she couldn't get anything right.

"Take your mess outside."

"It's hardly a mess," Sara exclaimed in an attempt to protect Clemmie from Sally's meanness.

Clemmie hurried out the door to where she could thump the erasers as much as she wanted and no one would complain about the dust.

"Speaking of messes," Sally returned archly, "is your costume ready for the party tomorrow night, Felicity?"

Costumes for the Harvest Party were a matter of great concern and rivalry among all the girls. Each year they tried to outdo their own previous efforts and show themselves off to advantage. Those who sewed beautifully made sure everyone else could see it. Those who couldn't went to great lengths to cover up the deficiency.

"Thank you for asking," said Felicity, countering Sally's rudeness with deliberate politeness. "I'm just about finished. I just have to tack a shimmery train onto the back, and then I'm done." The piece of shimmery material was what Mrs. Lawson had been saving for Felicity at the store.

As Sally's mother did not encourage such frivolities as fancy costumes, Felicity knew this would get Sally's goat. While Felicity kept on cleaning the blackboard, Sally digested Felicity's information to see what she could glean from it for herself. After a while, she stopped sweeping.

"Well, I was going to ask you if you could help me with mine, because I knew you'd finish your costume at least a week in advance."

Sally was unable even to ask for help without being snide. Felicity only shook out her cloth, deciding that, since her own costume was so beautiful, she could afford to be generous to the less fortunate.

"I'll help you if I can. Why don't you come over to my house in the morning. We'll finish them together."

"We'd be delighted to, wouldn't we, Jane?"

Sally did little without Jane Spry along. Without even asking Felicity, she made sure Jane was coming to Felicity's house too.

"Good," said Felicity. "I promised Clemmie I'd help her with hers as well."

Sally pulled down the corners of her mouth.

"Oh, don't invite Clemmie."

"Why not?" demanded Sara, who liked Clemmie a great deal and had seen how Sally had sabotaged Clemmie's speech.

"Well, you know...she's such a goody-goody," Sally drawled, "And there isn't a more ordinary, whiny person in the whole world than her."

"And all her *sighs*," Jane added, with her own exaggerated sigh, from across the room. "Oh, it gets on my nerves."

Felicity drew the line at being told who to invite to her own house.

"Clemmie always tags along with us. And I just couldn't see not letting her come now. Besides, she's already been invited."

To show the matter was closed, Felicity turned squarely back to the blackboard. Sally and Jane grimaced sourly at her shoulder blades. Before they could straighten out their faces, Felicity leaned round and caught them at it.

"Clemmie is an excellent seamstress. She could probably even help you with your costume."

Sally's retort was forestalled by Clemmie herself, who now came back in carrying the well-beaten erasers.

"So, have you decided on a costume, yet, Clemmie?" Sally asked.

"Yes, I'm going as a milkmaid."

"A milkmaid," mimicked Jane. "Well, at least you're bound to be the only one."

Clemmie's lip quivered. She was younger and smaller than the other girls in the room, and still badly shaken by her disastrous attempt at public speaking. The pig drawing still adorned Jane's slate, and it quite drained away Clemmie's will to fight back. Her distress aroused Sara, for Sara was fiercely loyal to those she considered her friends.

"Don't pay any attention to them, Clemmie. I think a milkmaid is very...wholesome."

By now, Felicity had finished the blackboard and put away the cloths and pail. The blackboard shone smooth and clean. She surveyed her work with satisfaction, for Felicity was nothing if not thorough.

"Well, that's good enough," Felicity declared. "Aunt Hetty is sure to think it's a perfect job.

Besides, I have to get to the general store before it gets dark. See you in the morning."

"If you still want our help..." Sara added tartly as she stowed the duster and pulled on her hat to leave with Felicity.

The two had no sooner reached the door than Clemmie realized she was about to be left alone with a Potts and a Spry. Dropping the erasers hastily back on their ledge, she sped toward the back of the room.

"May I walk part of the way with you, Felicity?"

Clemmie had very nice brown eyes in an otherwise plain face, and they appealed openly for rescue.

"If you like, Clemmie," Felicity answered, feeling benevolent. Secretly, Felicity liked having Clemmie tag along. Clemmie's admiration for Felicity was simple and obvious, and Felicity would have been less than human if she hadn't been flattered by it. Clemmie regarded Felicity as poised, pretty, skilled and popular—everything she herself was not. Felicity liked to imagine that she was the ideal Clemmie aspired to when Clemmie thought about her future years.

Chapter Five

None of the girls invited to the King farmhouse intended to miss out on Felicity's offer to help with their costumes. Clemmie was a good seamstress but short on imagination. Sara was brimming with ideas but shaky when it came to putting the actual pieces together. Sally Potts and Jane Spry, of course, were there to see how much benefit they could wring out of the situation for themselves.

All the girls except Clemmie, who hadn't arrived yet, were gathered around the broad kitchen table. In farmhouses, everything of interest is done at the kitchen table, and the King table was now overflowing with yards of material, scissors, thread and businesslike sewing baskets. The costumes were nearly done, and a good thing too, since the Harvest Party was that very evening.

Felicity was working on her princess costume while Sara struggled to stitch beads along the edge of a flowered scarf she had managed to acquire from her Aunt Olivia, Hetty's younger sister. Dreaming of jingling tambourines and mysterious fortunes told around campfires, Sara meant to go as a Gypsy, and was giving her costume every exotic decoration she could find.

Across the table, Jane wondered how to get the frill straight on a Little Bo Peep outfit, while Sally tacked up the hem of what had once been an old red tablecloth. The tablecloth was being transformed into a cloak for Little Red Riding Hood. Sara had said nothing about this choice of costume, but privately thought Sally would always look as though she were wearing a tablecloth no matter how much help Felicity provided. Besides, Sally was going to have a tough time imitating a sweet, helpful girl thinking only about taking goodies to her sick grandmother.

"Should I show you my new locket?" Sally asked with cool casualness. "It's a birthday present from my uncle in Halifax."

"Her very rich uncle," Jane added, just to make sure everyone realized what a very fine, superior item the locket must be.

Felicity glanced briefly at the small gold locket hanging on a fine chain around Sally's neck.

"It's very attractive," Felicity conceded stiffly. She hated being forced into admiring anything belonging to a Potts.

Sally stopped playing with her locket and examined the tiara that was to crown Felicity's royal personage, a slender circlet with tiny rhinestone flowers rising to a graceful peak in the front. To the eyes of the girls at the table, it glittered with all the allure of real jewels. Sally, of course, wouldn't give Felicity the satisfaction of this compliment.

"Felicity, I would think you would get bored of always wearing the same costume year after year at the party," she said instead.

"I agree," echoed Jane, whose purpose in life, like Herschel's, was to reinforce anything her leader said. "I'd think you'd want to try something else for a change."

When Felicity hit upon a good thing, she never felt the urge to change it just for the sake of variety. The princess costume had turned out to be a resounding success and one that Felicity repeated happily year after year.

"Oh, I never get bored, because every single year I create a new costume, and this year it's going to be the best one ever. Besides..." she glanced significantly at the red cloak that was still, despite all Sally's efforts, managing to look as though it needed dinner plates. "...you could still go as a princess if you cared to."

This broad hint bounced right off Sally. Perhaps Sally realized that, even if she tried, she would only succeed in looking like a toad with ambitions hopelessly above its station.

"Hardly. I would never dream of going as a princess if you were."

Having sneaked in another dig at Felicity, Sally now turned her attention to Sara.

"Sara, I see you're planning to go as a Gypsy. How very...unusual," she said, adding just enough of a pause before her last word to imply that the Gypsy costume was openly freakish.

As if she hadn't heard a word, Sara kept right on stitching. Irritated, Sally slipped on her Red Riding Hood cloak and swished about the kitchen to see if it hung properly.

"Mind you," said Jane to Sara, "given that you don't really have a home to call your own, a Gypsy seems so appropriate."

Sara's mother had died when she was three, and her father had recently sent her from Montreal to stay with her King relatives while he tried to clear his name in a business scandal. Sara's father had been rich, so Sara had arrived in Avonlea with dainty manners, a trunkful of dresses from Paris and a nanny of her own. Hetty King had dispatched the nanny pretty quickly, but the dresses and the manners had remained. Sally Potts had never got over being envious.

Sara held up the Gypsy bandana so she could

see how many more beads she would have to sew on. The light of battle was beginning to gleam in her eyes.

"Don't you think you'd be better off going as a wolf," she suggested to Sally, "rather than Red Riding Hood?"

Sensing a scrap about to start, Jane moved in quickly to divert attention. She was a good lieutenant, and there was no telling what Sara Stanley might do when roused.

"I, for one, can't wait to see Clemmie's milkmaid costume. She's bound to look more like a cow than a milkmaid."

"I don't know why she's decided to go in the first place," put in Sally, jumping on this new bandwagon. "She always has an awful time. Remember last year, how she just sat beside the refreshment table all night?"

Sara began to look even more belligerent. Belittling cracks weren't fair when Clemmie wasn't in the room to defend herself.

"I'll bet she was a lot more comfortable there than she would have been with you. She's a lot more sincere than you'll ever be."

"Ouch!" Attacked directly, Sally forgot what she was doing and jabbed her own finger with her needle. Of course, she had to take this out on Clemmie too.

"Well, in my books," she sputtered, "Clemmie's just a plain, ordinary old bore, and nothing's ever going to change that."

Felicity started to frown at this unflattering description of her friend. She, herself, had often been bothered by Clemmie's awkwardness and thought something should be done about it. Now an idea popped to the surface.

"I don't agree with that, girls. I read in the *Family Guide* that any girl, even the most ordinary, can be made to stand out in a crowd. With a little work, Clemmie could sparkle."

Jane and Sally simultaneously burst out laughing, as if this were the funniest idea they had heard that week.

"Clemmie sparkle?" Jane cackled. "It would take the entire Milky Way to make her shine!"

This was certainly rubbing Felicity's fur the wrong way. Felicity was a great believer in self-improvement. There was practically nothing a girl couldn't achieve, she thought, if she set her mind to it. Jane and Sally, in particular, she thought, could do with a lot of work in the self-improvement department.

"I don't think so. Clemmie's got a lot of potential. A change of hairstyle, perhaps, and a new costume...I could make her one of the most popular girls in Avonlea."

Even for Felicity, this was a pretty rash claim. Sally's eyes opened up very wide.

"Don't give yourself airs, Felicity King."

Instantly, without even thinking about what she was getting herself into, Felicity responded to the challenge.

"I'll bet I can."

Chapter Six

I'll bet I can! These were the four little words that started so much trouble in Felicity King's life that Saturday.

Sally's lips twitched madly as she tried to suppress her glee at Felicity's fatal slip. It wasn't often that Sally got Felicity King backed into this kind of corner, and she meant to take swift advantage of it.

"Would you bet your tiara?" Sally inquired tauntingly, her greedy eyes on the brilliant decoration. "I think I'd make a beautiful princess myself."

Felicity was not so far gone as to bet with a Potts without getting proper security.

"What would you bet?" she asked hotly.

"My locket."

Jane Spry sucked in a scandalized breath. "You can't bet your gold locket!"

Sally turned boastfully to her friend, certain she was on to a sure thing.

"Don't worry, Jane. I won't lose it. Felicity could never win this bet."

"That's what you think!" Felicity shot back, beginning to get genuinely steamed up.

"Well then, if you're so smart, Felicity King, why don't you try it? I'll bet you my locket for your tiara that Clemmie doesn't change a bit."

At this point, Felicity began to realize she might have boxed herself into a bit of a tight corner. When she hesitated, Jane Spry leaped in.

"In order for you to win, Clemmie would have to fit in at the party, have a wonderful time and maybe even get asked to dance."

This was a tall order, but Felicity could see no way to get out of it now with her pride intact.

"All right, then, I accept!"

On flinging herself recklessly into the bet, Felicity at least had the sense to snatch her tiara away from Sally Potts's grasping fingers. Determined to get it eventually, Sally set out the terms of winning—all in her own favor, of course.

"Jane will judge the winner at the end of the party," she declared.

Sara had been listening to the exchange in growing consternation. She flung down her Gypsy scarf.

"Don't be ridiculous, Felicity. It will be a one-sided contest. Besides, that's a mean thing to do to Clemmie. Clemmie doesn't need you to improve her. I certainly wouldn't let you try to change me."

"Well, maybe you'd be advised to consider it," Sally tossed at Sara, giving the multi-colored Gypsy costume another supercilious glance.

Seeing Sara swell up with indignation, Felicity leaped up from the table and hauled her away through the archway, where they couldn't easily be heard by Jane or Sally.

"Look, Sara," she said in a low, stubborn voice, "I only want to help Clemmie. She could even borrow my costume from last year. Now, you just have to promise you won't tell her what we're doing, and then I'll ease her into the costume, and she won't know what's happening to her."

Sara freed her arm from Felicity's grasp. She had strong principles in matters such as this. Beside, no good could ever come of trying to get the better of a Potts.

"I won't have any part of this."

"Then don't," cried Jane, whose sharp ears had caught the vehement exclamation.

Sally's gaze raked Sara up and down. She was determined to get rid of all opposition to the scheme. She wanted the tiara—and, most of all, she wanted to beat Felicity King.

"Well, Miss High-and-mighty, with all your principles, maybe you shouldn't even attend the party if you feel so strongly about it."

Sally was overjoyed at the prospect of taunting Sara Stanley out of going to the Harvest Party. People liked Sara and gave her far too much attention, Sally thought—an outrageous offence from a newcomer, dropped without a by-your-leave among the people of Avonlea.

By now, Sara had her temper up, and she fell straight into Sally's trap. Back she marched to the table. With a single motion, she gathered her costume up in her arms disdainfully.

"I don't intend to!"

Success made Sally's eyes dance. She pressed on, knowing just how to prod Sara into keeping her resolution.

"Don't worry, Felicity," Sally proclaimed loftily. "Sara's all talk and no action—not like us three."

"Oh, really?"

Sara took action at once. Turning on her heel,

she stormed out the door that led to the summer kitchen. She was gone before Felicity realized what was happening.

Felicity ran after her.

"Sara, you *have* to come to the party!"

The door slammed shut behind Felicity, leaving Sally and Jane snickering in triumph.

"My, that girl does have a temper," Jane enunciated in a mocking, falsetto voice.

Sally let out an equally mocking sigh. "And all because Felicity's trying to help poor Clemmie."

"Tsk!"

Out in the summer kitchen, Sara was swiftly packing her costume into the carpetbag she had brought it over in. The summer kitchen was at the back of the house, and that was where the farm family cooked and put up preserves in the summer to prevent roasting everyone out of the main house with the heat from the roaring wood stove. Felicity had both her hands raised in a half-pleading, half-aggravated gesture. It was unthinkable that Sara shouldn't come to the Harvest Party.

"Sara...listen!"

Sara snapped the carpetbag shut. "Clemmie looks up to you, Felicity. She always has. The way those two speak to your face, I can only imagine what they say behind your back."

In the main kitchen, Jane and Sally hopped up from their chairs to peer out the window.

"Look," cried Jane, "there's Clemmie now."

Chuckling to herself, Jane turned towards the door Felicity had just gone through.

"Felicity, go and get your old costume out of the mothballs."

"And," Sally called in a loud voice, "Sara Stanley, don't you breathe a word!"

The voices came through, loud and clear. Sara glowered at Felicity.

"I'll have nothing to do with a gang of two-faced jellyfish."

Colorful descriptions like this didn't go very far toward cooling the argument. Two bright red spots appeared on Felicity's cheeks, and she immediately abandoned her efforts to make Sara see reason.

"Well, I'm going to get out my costume," she snapped right back, not in the least resembling a jellyfish.

True to her word, Felicity sped up the stairs in search of the outfit. She had no sooner vanished than Clemmie trudged through the back door into the summer kitchen, carrying a crumpled bag that had her costume in it.

"Hello, Sara," she ventured, not sure why Sara was looking so stirred up and stiff.

No sooner had she opened her mouth than Sally and Jane appeared in the summer kitchen too, hats and coats on, clearly on their way out.

"Clemmie! Hi!"

The voices of the two girls slopped over with sugar, as if they had been waiting all day just to welcome Clemmie.

"How are you?" Sally inquired, managing to sound as though she was actually interested.

"Hello, Jane. Hello, Sally," Clemmie returned, a little uncertain at all the sudden warmth from the same people who had yesterday caused her so much embarrassment. "I know I'm a little late but..."

"We're so delighted you could join us." Sally put an arm around Clemmie. "Felicity can't wait to see your costume. She'll be right down."

Nodding towards the inner door, Sara picked up her bag with a jerk.

"If you had any sense at all, you wouldn't go in there."

Poor Clemmie stared in confusion into the main kitchen, which looked perfectly harmless to her.

"Why?"

"Oh, you know Sara," Sally interjected hurriedly

lest Sara spill everything. "She always gets worked up into these big huffs over nothing."

Sally and Jane started to walk towards the door to the yard. Clemmie grew ever more mixed up.

"Aren't you staying?"

Clemmie had looked forward to a sewing party. Sally patted the red cloak folded under her arm.

"No, we finished already. We'll see you all later on tonight. Bye now. Come along, Sara."

Before Sara could defend herself, Sally grasped her by the arm and hauled her bodily from the King farmhouse. Sara was taken completely by surprise.

"Take my advice and leave," Sara yelled over her shoulder to Clemmie as she struggled with Sally and tried to hold on to her carpetbag.

"Felicity will only be mean to you."

"What?"

Clemmie hadn't heard because Jane slammed the outside door shut practically in Clemmie's face.

"Let go of me!" Sara hissed, twisting loose from Sally's iron grip.

Sally let go willingly. It didn't matter now how many objections Sara had. Once outside the King farmhouse, she had no choice but to go on home and leave Clemmie to her fate.

Chapter Seven

Ten-year-old Cecily came in from the barn, where she had been gathering eggs, to join Clemmie and Felicity. The two sisters watched as Clemmie lifted her milkmaid costume out of the wrinkled bag she had brought it in. Held up against Clemmie for everyone to see, the rustic costume turned out to be surprisingly nice.

"Did you really make it all yourself?" Felicity asked, impressed in spite of herself by the wide, puffed sleeves, pretty, trimmed skirt and airy white cap. Clemmie was usually so bumbling that it always came as a surprise when she did something well. Her sewing was one of the few things Clemmie was proud of.

"I worked on it for ages," Clemmie confessed. Anxiously, she looked at Felicity to see what Felicity thought. Felicity was the final judge of fashion in Clemmie's eyes. Felicity's approval was all Clemmie wanted in the world.

"Well, it is very nice. Certainly the best-looking milkmaid costume that I've ever seen."

"It is?"

Clemmie turned pink with pleasure, not

thinking to calculate just how many milkmaid's costumes Felicity was likely to have seen.

Felicity hesitated, looking regretfully at all Clemmie's hard work. The milkmaid costume would certainly suit Clemmie, adding just the needed simplicity and charm to Clemmie's awkward ways. Then Felicity caught sight of her own tiara lying on the table, twinkling at her mockingly. If Clemmie went to the Harvest Party as an ordinary milkmaid, Sally Potts would get her fat paws permanently on the lovely thing. Felicity just had to win the bet.

"But it's not nearly as becoming as a princess," she said carefully. "You're sure to be much more popular if you arrive as royalty. You'd sparkle!"

Clemmie smiled in rueful disbelief. "I could never sparkle."

"Of course you could," Felicity assured her, with all the conviction of the *Family Guide* in her words. The *Family Guide* was a magazine that came once a month and, even in the remotest farmhouses, served as the arbiter of fashion, dispenser of domestic advice and source of ideas for improvement projects such as Felicity was even then undertaking.

Reaching behind her, Felicity produced her own costume from the year before. Felicity had devoted much labor to it, and it was the very image of a princess's gown, sweeping to the floor in long, majestic folds. A short satin cape fell softly over the shoulders gleaming richly. Clemmie remembered vividly how everyone had admired Felicity in it.

"You can borrow my costume from last year. It would be perfect."

Felicity held the costume up where the sunshine streaming through the window struck it and turned it into glowing cascades of color before Clemmie's dazzled eyes. The costume hovered before Clemmie like a lustrous temptation, quite overpowering the milkmaid outfit. Clemmie had never dreamed that Felicity would lend her anything so elaborate, and the possibility quite turned her head.

"Really?"

Clemmie saw herself sweeping into the Town Hall, almost like a real princess. She could imagine everyone wanting to admire her and talk to her. Unfortunately, she was seeing herself as Felicity, with all her poise and grace, would look. In her heart of hearts, she feared that she might be nothing more than a hesitant impostor in a borrowed gown.

"But what if it doesn't fit?" Clemmie wanted

to know. Clemmie was considerably smaller and younger than Felicity. She had an anxious vision of the hem trailing on the floor and the waist of the dress down near her knees.

"Don't worry," Felicity muttered determinedly. "I'll make it fit."

The farmhouse kitchen had big windows and just outside them, on the porch, Felix was stacking wood. He used the opportunity to peer inside to see what was happening with his sisters and Clemmie. The things girls did were often incomprehensible to him and quite hilarious. He forgot about the wood and stopped to enjoy the show. Inside, Felicity was coaching Clemmie on how to sparkle.

Felicity had Clemmie standing in the middle of the kitchen, and she was wagging her finger at her.

"Now, Clemmie, if you want to look like a princess, you have to act like one. Cecily, hand me that book."

Neither Felicity, Cecily nor Clemmie noticed Felix's amused face against the window pane. Cecily picked up the heavy copy of *the Farmer's Home Veterinarian*, which always sat atop the mantel, and handed it to her sister. Felicity placed the book on top of Clemmie's head, then moved across the room to stand facing her, and beckoned her to come. Fearful of dropping the book, Clemmie began to walk slowly across the room towards her instructor.

"Head erect," Felicity ordered. "Keep your eyes up. Shoulders back—good!"

Clemmie did her very best, but only a real princess could have balanced so massive a book on her head all the way across the room. Without warning, right beside the stove, the book slipped off Clemmie's head and crashed with a thump to the floor. Cecily dashed to retrieve it, and Felicity tried not to lose heart. Transforming Clemmie into a paragon of grace and elegance was proving much more difficult than the *Family Guide* had led her to believe.

"Don't worry, Clemmie, just try it again. Remember now, practice makes perfect."

Felicity put the book on Clemmie's head again. Clemmie set out to repeat her shaky walk, getting somewhat further this time. Felicity brightened.

"That's better, Clemmie!"

"You really think so?"

Clemmie barely dared move her lips to ask the question. She'd had no idea being a princess was such hard work, and she was developing troublesome doubts about her own ability in the royalty department.

"Yes," assured Felicity quickly, lest Clemmie give up and ruin everything, "but keep your shoulders back—you're all hunched over."

Clemmie's shoulders were hunched, mostly from effort. When she tried to straighten them, the book plummeted to the floor again and fell open to "Diseases of Sheep." It wouldn't stand many more trips to the linoleum before the spine cracked and one of the adult Kings got very annoyed about it.

Chapter Eight

Outside, Felix motioned urgently. Edward Ray, who had been using his sister as an excuse to visit the King farm, ran up onto the porch too.

"You won't believe your eyes," Felix whispered, giggling. "Felicity's doing the stupidest thing."

What they saw now was Clemmie seated at the kitchen table with a mirror propped up in front of her. Felicity was busily brushing Clemmie's loosened hair. The one thing Clemmie did have in abundance was thick, luxuriant toffee-colored hair.

"You're going to have to wear your hair up," Felicity told her, smoothing the heavy tresses.

"You could easily be a Gibson Girl. Your hair goes on forever."

The Gibson Girl style was all the rage at the moment. Every magazine, newspaper and song-sheet featured a girl with her hair in a knot on top of her head, the clever upsweep making it look twice as luxuriant as it actually was.

"Are you going to wear yours up?" Clemmie asked uncertainly. In this princess business, she needed to take every cue from Felicity.

"No, I've decided to wear it down this year. Then we won't look exactly the same."

Clemmie looked positively rapturous at the idea that people might see any resemblance between herself and Princess Felicity. Cecily picked up the flashing tiara Felicity was planning to wear and placed it on her own head. Clemmie picked up last year's tiara and examined it reverently.

"This tiara is beautiful," she exclaimed, even though it was far less glamorous than the one Cecily wore.

"My mother helped me make that one last year," Felicity said complacently. The glue has held pretty well."

Clemmie's mother, Mrs. Ray, was famous for her strictness and would never have held with such nonsense as making tiaras. Clemmie had

had to work on her costume very quietly, and she often envied the freedoms of the easygoing King household. Felicity pointed to the new tiara Cecily was modeling.

"I bought this one from a costume catalogue, but my old one still has its sparkle, doesn't it?"

"Oh, yes."

Felicity placed the older tiara on Clemmie's head, where it sat winking in the sunlight.

"Oh," Felicity sighed in ecouraging admiration, "you're going to look so fashionable. Well, we might as well try on the costume now. I can play with your hair later."

Edward and Felix were still at their posts, and not much wood was getting stacked. Felix started to laugh but Edward stopped him with a sharp poke. He had no intention of missing anything Felicity might be involved in.

"Felicity tries to be so bossy," Felix muttered. Felicity did queen it over her younger sister and brother, and Felix had often had to struggle manfully not to be downtrodden.

Edward could barely smother his own merriment. "I like the way her ears turn red when she's ordering people around," he whispered.

Eventually, even the boys lost interest as Felicity set about altering the costume to fit Clemmie. After much tucking and shortening, Clemmie tried it on. The costume had a close-fitting bodice on the outside that laced up from top to bottom. In order to get the proper effect, the bodice had to be laced as snugly as possible. Felicity accomplished this by bracing her knee against Clemmie and tugging on the laces with all her might. As Cecily fluffed out the folds of the short, supple cape, Felicity gave a final, enormous jerk on the laces. Clemmie, shocked at the tortures princesses found themselves subjected to, gasped aloud.

"It's too tight, Felicity. I can hardly breathe."

Ignoring Clemmie's protest, Felicity tied the laces into an elaborate bow and stood back.

"There," she said, quite satisfied.

Clemmie was still gasping in short, desperate breaths. A most unbecoming purple shade climbed her cheeks.

"Oh, it's too tight!—I'll never be able to wear it in public."

"It's fine," Felicity informed her forcefully. She implied that princesses suffered cheerfully for their beauty and Clemmie was being ungrateful to protest.

Clemmie's face tightened in distress.

"I'll never be able to get it on. It's too embarrassing."

❧❧❧

Jane continued to flash the pig picture and make grunting noises. She was quickly joined by Sally Potts, who did an even better pig imitation than Jane.

❧❧❧❧

Clemmie's distress aroused Sara, for Sara was fiercely
loyal to those she considered her friends.
"Don't pay any attention to them, Clemmie.
I think a milkmaid is very ... wholesome."

❧❧❧

Felicity was busily brushing Clemmie's loosened hair.
"You're going to have to wear your hair up,"
Felicity told her, smoothing the heavy tresses.
"You could easily be a Gibson Girl.
Your hair goes on forever."

❧

Sally turned to Jane, giggling. "Oh, and she can talk,
too. It's a wonder she can breathe
in that tight-fitting frock."
A red stain climbed Clemmie's cheeks.
Now, because of Sally, she became doubly
self-conscious about how tight the bodice was.

As Clemmie struggled to expand her rib cage, Felicity saw a bracing speech was needed on the spot to keep Clemmie's resolution up. It would be intolerable to lose her bet to Sally Potts.

"Nonsense, you're going to have to wear it, and that's all there is to it, because I'm not going to help you finish your milkmaid costume now. I really want this party to be something special for you, Clemmie. It will be the first social step in the right direction that you've ever taken. But you have to have faith in yourself if you want to be popular."

Cecily stood up on a chair holding the mirror so Clemmie could see herself. Felicity fixed the tiara in Clemmie's hair, while Clemmie inspected the unfamiliar image that gleamed back at her from the glass. The mirror was too small for Clemmie to see the complete costume, only bits of the shiny material rippling as she moved. Though the hem was still dragging on the floor and the bodice slowly suffocating her in its iron grip, Clemmie imagined the costume to be as beautiful as it had been when Felicity had held it up in the light.

Dragging in another constricted breath, Clemmie tried very hard—and found she could have faith. The faith was not in herself but in Felicity. She even managed to smile. After all, if Felicity promised her a wonderful time in the princess costume, then she would have a wonderful time. Gratitude welled up in Clemmie's breast.

"Oh, Felicity," Clemmie exclaimed, not even stopping to wonder why Felicity looked so uneasy, "you're such a good friend!"

Clemmie wriggled out of the costume and scooted home in a haze of happy anticipation. Watching her go, Felicity was troubled in her conscience—and not only on Clemmie's account. As soon as Clemmie was out of sight, Felicity pulled on her hat and coat and dashed down the lane to Rose Cottage, where Sara lived with Aunt Hetty and Aunt Olivia. Sara had become Felicity's closest friend since she had arrived in Avonlea, and her approval meant a good deal to Felicity. She just had to have another try at making a convincing case for her scheme.

Aunt Hetty, answering the knock on the door at Rose Cottage, looked at a pink-faced and breathless Felicity with some surprise.

"Felicity King, I'd have thought you'd be getting ready for the party."

Too distracted to answer, Felicity stepped in and started taking off her hat and coat.

"I need to talk to Sara, Aunt Hetty."

"Oh, she's in the parlor...moping." Hetty gestured behind her in bewilderment. "I can't fathom it. She's dying to go one minute, refusing the next."

Hetty's life had always been run with order and predictability. Since Sara's arrival, the girl's mercurial temperament and passionate emotions had been a trial and a mystery.

"Maybe," Felicity said worriedly, "I can convince her."

Felicity had hoped that Sara would be over her huff by now. The fact that Sara was still refusing to go to the Harvest Party was not a good omen at all.

In the parlor, Sara sat curled up on the big horsehair sofa, her nose buried in a book. The crystal ball she had meant to carry as a Gypsy fortune-teller lay abandoned on the table beside her. The rest of her costume was nowhere in evidence. Felicity stepped in and stood looking at her cousin in the midst of the parlor's sepulchral hush.

"Hello, Sara."

Hearing Felicity's voice, Sara didn't even look up, though her nose rose slightly in the air.

"I'll have nothing to do with you if you're still

bent on the idea of deceiving Clemmie, just to stay friends with frog-face Sally Potts."

When Sara made up her mind about something, she was practically impossible to budge. Felicity walked across the rug and sat down in the hard-backed chair opposite Sara. She, too, could be stubborn when she made up her mind.

"I'll have you know that Clemmie Ray is very appreciative for all that I've done. She's shown much more confidence than she's ever shown before."

If Felicity thought this argument was going to sway Sara, she was wrong.

"You don't fool me, Felicity. Once Clemmie finds out about this, it will be on your head," Sara said ominously.

"She'll never find out," Felicity insisted. "And you'll see that I was right to help her when everyone at the party is impressed."

Sara buried herself more deeply in her reading. The book cover was big enough to hide a good part of her face, which was now scowling.

"Please leave, then. I'm not having anything to do with this."

Felicity would bend her own pride only so far. When she saw that nothing less than total renunciation of the bet with Sally Potts would satisfy

Sara, Felicity stood up abruptly. It was too late to back out, and she would not have Sally Potts and Jane Spry gloating for the rest of the winter over the tiara. Clemmie, Felicity decided, would make a creditable princess if it were the last thing Felicity did. Then Sara would be forced to change her mind. Setting her jaw, Felicity turned her back on Sara and marched straight back out the door.

Chapter Nine

As soon as dusk fell, buggies loaded with people began to pull up at the door of the Avonlea Town Hall, and the Harvest Party began. Warm yellow light streamed through the doors and windows, and fiddle music made feet tap before they even got inside. Avonlea was working itself into a festive mood.

Things were well under way when Alec King and his wife, Janet, pulled up in the buggy with the children. Felix had gone ahead earlier with one of his school friends, hoping to be first to the refreshment table. Cecily, wearing a flowered hand-me-down dress of Felicity's, with flowers in her hair and carrying a bouquet, was Mary, Mary, Quite Contrary.

Clemmie had come over to Felicity's to get dressed, and both girls had their coats on over their princess costumes. As they entered the Town Hall vestibule, Clemmie looked around in excitement and trepidation at the scene where her life was to be transformed for the better.

"Oh, Felicity, my stomach is all butterflies."

Actually, her stomach felt more like it was all bullfrogs and jackrabbits thumping around trying to get out. Clemmie had had no idea it would be so nerve-wracking to be on the verge of overwhelming popularity and never-ending fun.

Janet King, her toes already itching to dance, turned to the girls. Never suspecting Felicity's motives, she had been pleased with what she thought was a fine gesture of generosity towards Clemmie.

"Let us take your coats girls."

"Yes," said Alec. "We'll hang 'em up, and you can get yourselves ready to make a grand entrance."

Like the proud, indulgent parents they were, the two grown-ups stood admiring the costumes for a moment, then went towards the cloakroom.

"Good luck," Janet called out to the girls over her burden of coats and hats.

This was it. Clemmie was about to be cast into

the thick of the social whirl. And luck was what they were going to need, Felicity thought. Clemmie was starting to look as shaky as she had when she'd tried to give her speech. Apprehensively, Clemmie turned to her mentor.

"What should I do?"

If ever there was a time for encouragement, it was now. Felicity straightened Clemmie's tiara, which had an infuriating tendency to slip sideways, even though Clemmie's hair was up in a Gibson Girl knot. Felicity's own hair hung in a shining fall down her back and her new tiara glittered with gratifying brilliance each time she moved her head.

"Now, just remember what I've told you. You've got to be outgoing and friendly if you want to be well-liked. Then the butterflies will all go away."

In spite of her fervent resolve to have faith in Felicity's assurances, Clemmie looked doubtful. How exactly did one go about being outgoing and friendly?

"I never know what to say," she confessed plaintively. Getting tongue-tied just when she most needed to talk was one of Clemmie's worst problems.

Felicity couldn't imagine being stuck for words. After all, there were thousands and thousands of them in the world. She put together a few of the simplest.

"All you've got to say is, `Hello, how are you? Isn't it a lovely gathering?' And then, you'll see, the conversation will just take off from there."

So that's all it took! Why hadn't anyone told her ages before? Clemmie immediately latched on tight to the magic phrases.

"How are you?" she repeated. "Isn't it a lovely gathering?"

Felicity and Cecily exchanged a pained glance. In the wooden way Clemmie spoke, there wasn't the least evidence of sparkle.

"How are you? Isn't it a lovely gathering?" Clemmie tried again, still as wooden, only louder. It seemed beyond her to modulate her voice and remember her phrases at the same time.

Felicity forced a bright smile. It was clear that Clemmie wasn't going to get any better with practice. They had better get to enjoying the party right away.

"Now, are you ready to make your grand entrance?" Felicity asked briskly.

Clemmie swallowed hard and nodded her head. Balling her clammy palms into fists, Clemmie gamely followed Felicity and Cecily into the Town Hall.

Just inside the inner door, Edward, dressed in a pirate costume, leaped in front of them. Trust Edward to spot Felicity instantly and start making a nuisance of himself.

"*En garde!*" he cried, brandishing a sword made of an old piece of lath wrapped in silver paper.

Edward wore a three-cornered hat, a black eyepatch and a great lopsided black mustache painted on his upper lip. He looked about as fearsome as Edward Ray could be made to look, but Felicity pushed his sword away without a word. She had much more important matters at hand than treating with pirates.

Most of Avonlea was in the Town Hall, and the interior was full of knots and swirls of people all bent on enjoying themselves. The three girls, being shorter than the adults, were peering about, trying to sort out all the activity. They had barely escaped from Edward when they all but ran into Harmon Andrews. Harmon was one of the many grown-ups helping with the festivities. He beamed down genially at the two princesses and at Cecily's garlands.

"Ladies!" he exclaimed gallantly, "you look beautiful."

At this hopeful sign, Clemmie flushed and

Felicity nodded regally. They made their way past a table filled with baked goods and festooned with red and blue ribbons from the earlier judging of the baking competition. Beyond it, several children, all in costume, were milling excitedly around. Games were being organized in one corner and there was much anticipation in that direction. Cecily, who was more interested in games and prizes than social triumphs, ran off to join the fun.

Felix, dressed as a tramp, bumped into his sister.

"Hey, want to play 'Pin The Tail On The Donkey'?"

This wasn't a proposal to make to a princess.

"Not right now," Felicity told her brother, continuing on her way with Clemmie in her wake.

A buoyant atmosphere filled the hall. On the stage, fiddlers played, tapping their feet and sawing their bows. A huge wheelbarrow filled with apples, Indian corn and pumpkins sat at the front of the stage, illustrating the theme of a bountiful harvest. Nearby, a long refreshment table loaded with punch, cake, cookies and coffee sat tempting the appetites of everyone who looked at it.

Felicity, imitated by Clemmie, waved to several people as they made their way through the room. Judson Parker could be seen glad-handing his way through the hall, closely followed by the ever-faithful Herschel. The girls stopped beside a group of men spinning a carnival wheel and shouting with laughter as their numbers came up winners or losers. The dance floor was already filling up with couples. And, inevitably Sally Potts, alias Little Red Riding Hood, followed by Jane Spry dressed as Bo Peep, found Felicity and Clemmie.

"Isn't it a lovely gathering?" Clemmie was saying to a startled woman nearby. "How are you?"

"Well, if it isn't Clemmie Ray," Jane chortled. "What on earth are you wearing?" she exclaimed with feigned shock.

With exaggerated care, Sally turned to her companion.

"Jane, she's a milkmaid—can't you tell? Milkmaids always wear hand-me-downs."

Naturally, Sally and Jane tried to upset Clemmie as much as possible, all to win the bet. Clemmie had no inkling of this, and her face fell because they didn't seem to recognize her splendid gown.

"I decided to come as a princess instead," Clemmie felt forced to tell them. If they couldn't tell she was a princess, even wearing a tiara, perhaps nobody else could either. The first great cloud of doubt sailed into Clemmie's evening.

Sally turned to Jane, giggling.

"Oh, and she can talk, too. It's a wonder she can breathe in that tight-fitting frock."

A red stain climbed Clemmie's cheeks. Felicity had laced the costume even more tightly than she had when Clemmie first tried it on. The bodice held in a tucked-up waist, which made the costume small enough and short enough for Clemmie to wear. If the laces came loose, it might all fall down. Clemmie felt like a poker inside it, and she'd been afraid to tell Felicity that she could only breathe in tiny, constricted breaths. Now, because of Sally, she became doubly self-conscious about how tight the bodice was.

"I can't wait to see her bob for apples in it," Jane snickered.

Felicity saw she had better get her charge away quickly or risk the collapse of Clemmie's nerve altogether. She grabbed her companion's elbow.

"Come on, Clemmie."

As fast as she could, Felicity steered Clemmie away from the demoralizing influence of Jane and Sally.

Ten steps on, they found themselves in the

middle of another group of merrymakers. Clemmie, rattled now, began rapidly to recite the speech that would make her sparkle.

"Isn't it a lovely gathering?" she said to the right and to the left. "How are you this evening...? Isn't it a lovely gathering?"

Since Clemmie singled out no one in particular to address those words to, and since she sounded as though she were wound up mechanically, all she got for her efforts were a lot of astonished looks and not a few suppressed giggles. Appalled at how even the simplest greeting could go so awry, Felicity hauled Clemmie on past the table where the pie-tasting was taking place.

After the judging was over, the goods entered in the baking contest were sliced up and doled out among the most discriminating palates in Avonlea. This was considered by many to be an even stiffer test than the judging itself. Janet King found herself at the end of the table having a slice of mincemeat pie handed to her by Mrs. Potts. Mrs. Potts fancied herself quite a cook, but she was the only one in town who did. Janet bit reluctantly into the pie and barely suppressed a shudder.

"Uh, just...how much mincemeat did you put in there, Mrs. Potts?"

"Enough to give you nightmares," Mrs. Potts returned jovially, never imagining that Janet thought the statement was actually the most apt description of the pie.

If the adults were interested in the pie-tasting, the children were interested in the apple-bob, which Harmon Andrews was supervising, standing over a barrel filled with water in which a great many rosy apples were bobbing. Several children were eagerly awaiting their turn to try to pick one out of the barrel with their mouths.

Harmon pointed to a boy.

"What about you? Are you going to try?"

Even as the boy was bent over at the waist, his hands behind his back, trying his best, Harmon noticed Felicity and beckoned to her. Harmon was a great admirer of princess costumes and Felicity was striking in her pale, flowing dress with the carefully attached shimmery train.

"Come on, Felicity, it's your turn."

Felicity glided over.

"Oh, I hope my hair doesn't get wet," she giggled.

Graceful as royalty, Felicity bent over the barrel delicately and came up with a glowing apple. She had cleverly grasped the stem in her teeth and barely got a drop of water on her in the process.

Everyone laughed approvingly as she lifted her head up with her prize. Behind her, Jane Spry and Sally Potts had quietly joined the group of children watching. Their eyes darted around to see what mischief they could cause.

"Well done, Felicity," Harmon congratulated her. "Now, that's about as perfect an apple as you could wish for, hmm? Who's next?"

Carried away by her success, Felicity pushed Clemmie forward. Apple-bobbing didn't require that one sparkle, or even talk. Here, surely, was something that Clemmie could do. "Come on, Clemmie, it's easy."

Scarcely able to move or breathe inside her bodice, Clemmie didn't think so at all. Her head filled up with a horrible image of the entire costume splitting open if she even thought about bending over. Head down, she sidled sideways, hoping to make herself invisible behind a wall of taller people. Before she had got five feet, she found her path to escape blocked by Jane Spry. Jane had a mean glint in her eye.

"We're all waiting, Clemmie."

Jane was bigger than Clemmie and looked as though she meant to hold onto her bodily if Clemmie tried to get away.

"Hurry up, Clemmie," Sally urged, coming up

on the other side of her quarry. "There's a line of others waiting."

Looking very unhappy, Clemmie moved up to the barrel sloshing with water and apples. As she bent over slowly, she felt every eye burning into her. The laces of the bodice cut deeply into her waist but the costume, thanks to Felicity's firm stitching, didn't split. Instead, Clemmie's tiara tumbled off with a plop and sank end over end right to the bottom of the barrel. Jane laughed hysterically at this fiasco and Sally looked tickled enough to burst.

"My tiara!" Clemmie squeaked as her hand flew to the top of her head. Her arm couldn't get all the way up because of the rigid pressure of the bodice, so Clemmie was left with her fingers jabbing the air and her face a stark sheet of mortification.

Taking pity on her, Harmon rolled up his sleeve, thrust his hand down and came up with the waterlogged crown.

"That's okay," he told Clemmie, handing it back to her. "Just give it a shake."

Clemmie didn't dare because of what the water might have done to the glue holding the stones in. There was nothing for it but to put the tiara, still dripping, back on her head and feel the cold drips encircling her scalp. As Jane and Sally sniggered maliciously, Clemmie bolted, instantly pursued by Felicity, who knew that if Clemmie got outside the hall and headed towards home, she might as well give up the bet then and there.

Chapter Ten

Avonlea people loved to dance, and soon the dance floor was filled with couples. Even Mrs. Potts had corralled a partner, but she insisted on leading him so strongly that he gave up on her, bowed gallantly and made his escape. Just as Mrs. Potts was looking about for another hapless individual to pounce upon, the tune ended, and several men close to Mrs. Potts looked privately relieved.

Before the fiddlers had a chance to launch into another song, Herschel hoisted himself up onto the platform and gestured for them to stop playing. Bows fell away from strings and boots stopped thumping. The villagers, though poised for their next dance, nevertheless stopped where they were and applauded politely. Herschel, who looked as though he enjoyed public speaking about as much as Clemmie, cleared his throat, shifted from foot to foot and finally began.

"Folks, uh, may I kindly have your attention, please? Ladies and gentlemen, quiet, please. Gather round, if you would."

For lack of a second choice, the crowd did begin to mill about a little and move towards the platform. Herschel held out his long, skinny arms in a beckoning gesture and cleared his throat again.

"I would like to introduce your soon-to-be-elected Member for the Legislative Assembly, Mr. Judson Parker."

This grandiose statement sounded twice as presumptuous coming out of Herschel's mouth. Quite a number of people looked skeptical about the "soon-to-be-elected" bit, but they applauded anyway. The people in the Town Hall were in a jolly mood and felt generous, even towards Herschel. Besides, Herschel himself led the applause.

Herschel scurried hastily aside as Judson Parker puffed up the steps and took the floor. Judson already had a slick sheen of perspiration over his face from the heat and activity inside the hall. The buttons of his jacket strained to contain his swelling stomach, and the green checks of his suit were so conspicuous that more than one observer wondered whether Judson's tailor had been instructed to steal the awnings from a grocery store. Judson grinned from ear to ear at all the upturned faces, each one of whom could have some part in handing him a vote.

"Thank you, thank you, thank you. I...I want to thank you all very much for your kind support of my candidacy in the upcoming election. And, uh, as a demonstration of my sincere appreciation, I have the pleasure of being able to donate a prize tonight to the young person wearing the best costume."

Best costume! An excited buzz ran through all the children in the room as they suddenly took an interest in politics. Among them were Clemmie and Felicity, who stood gazing up expectantly. Felicity had pooh-poohed Sally and Jane so much that Clemmie had taken heart again. Full of new hope, she had followed Felicity back into the midst of the fray. Now Clemmie twisted about, trying to get a clear view of Judson Parker, while a slow smile of assurance stole across Felicity's lips. There could be no doubt as to who had the best costume in the room—Princess Felicity, of course.

Whipping out a great white handkerchief to mop his brow, Judson smiled and waited for his announcement to sink in. The prize was one more clever part of his campaign plan. Children who won prizes were apt to have grateful parents— parents with a vote to cast.

"My assistant, Mr. Herschel, and I will be passing among you to determine which costume best deserves the award," Judson boomed out. "The prize will be two tickets for the winner and a guest to join me in my box at the Charlottetown Opera House to listen to and to meet that illustrious soprano, Nellie Melba..."

All around the hall, breaths whooshed in. This was much more of a prize than anyone had expected. Nellie Melba was a singer celebrated all over Europe and America. A famous French chef had even invented Melba Toast in her honor, in order to help her keep her waist slender. Peach Melba, also created to please her, was said to be her favorite dessert. Charlottetown restaurants were offering it on their menus to please her hordes of adoring fans.

"Oh, she's wonderful!" exclaimed Mrs. Lawson, who would make a valiant attempt at playing the piano whenever she was asked. She wished she were a girl again, just to get a chance at those tickets.

"...who will be appearing," Judson continued, just when the furor had started to die down, "for one night only in three weeks' time. Thank you very much."

Still mopping his brow, Judson lumbered back down into the crush of people. As he disappeared, she could hardly contain her excitement. Felicity adored anyone famous and fancied herself quite refined enough to appreciate all the finer points of the opera house.

"Can you imagine?" She turned to Clemmie. "She's a world-famous celebrity. They say it's impossible to get tickets."

Felicity had read wistfully about the performance only a few days before in the newspaper. Now, a glance downward at her own sweeping train made Felicity feel as though her ticket were already in her hand. And, before the concert, there would be the delicious process of choosing who her guest was to be. Everyone would be dying to go, of course, even pop-eyed Sally Potts. Felicity almost giggled aloud at the thought of Sally Potts begging to go along. Oh, if only Sara...

But Sara Stanley wasn't there to share this pleasure. Though she wouldn't admit it, even to herself, Felicity had been keeping an eye out for Sara ever since she had arrived, and Sara was definitely nowhere to be seen. And, knowing how stubborn Sara was, she'd probably still be angry with Felicity by the time the concert rolled around.

Oh, well, thought Felicity, squelching her disappointment. If Sara was going to remain that obstinate, she could hardly expect to be asked along to Charlottetown. Felicity didn't want to think about how much less fun the concert would be without Sara's cheerful company.

Clemmie, much calmed by Felicity, was still recovering from the apple-bobbing incident. True, the glue was starting to swell on the wet tiara, but since it was on top of Clemmie's head, Clemmie couldn't see this. She even managed to smile, just for one reckless second daring to imagine what it might be like to win the prize herself.

The fiddlers had taken their places and started up again. The dance floor quickly filled with dancers. Felicity straightened her own tiara, smoothed her train and set about looking as aristocratic as she could. She was just trying to find out where Mr. Parker and his assistant were when her gaze fell on a pirate swaggering purposefully in her direction. She stopped short and prodded Clemmie.

"Oh, no. Here comes your brother, the pest. I suppose I'll have to give him a dance."

Her dismay was not quite as real as her voice

made it sound. Pest or not, it was still flattering to have a boy want to dance with her—especially if that boy was Edward Ray. Felicity seemed prepared to face up to the ordeal for the next thing Clemmie knew, Edward was leading Felicity onto the dance floor and leaving Clemmie stranded by herself. Clemmie tried not to panic, telling herself that princesses had to be able to get along on their own.

Meanwhile, Felicity had her own motives for dancing with Edward, and had certainly not abandoned Clemmie's cause. To win the bet with Sally Potts *and* win the prize for best costume too would vindicate the evening completely for Felicity.

"Edward," Felicity said, after she had danced demurely halfway around the room with him, "I thought it would be nice for Clemmie to have a dance. Wouldn't one of your friends like to ask her?"

Getting Clemmie a dance with someone was one of the requirements for winning the bet. However, even despite Felicity's best smile, Edward wasn't proving cooperative.

"Don't be ridiculous," he snorted. "I'm here to enjoy myself, not take care of my little sister."

Felicity gritted her teeth behind her smile and tried not to sound pleading.

"You must have one friend who would like to dance with her. It's really important to me that Clemmie have a good time tonight."

She dared not explain just how important it was to her, for Edward would never let her forget it for weeks to come. He only grinned as wickedly as he could and said nothing in return, wallowing in the rare novelty of having Felicity talk to him in a civilized manner.

Chapter Eleven

Edward's delight, combined with Felicity's diplomatic expression, carried across the room to where Alec and Janet King stood beside the punch bowl, cooling themselves with a drink and beaming at the dancers. They had been dancing too, proving to the astonished youngsters that an old married couple could still kick up their heels.

"Oh, Alec," Janet chuckled, "Felicity's so excited about the contest. She's sure she's going to win. You know, I can't help but admire Mr. Parker's generosity."

Alec stopped with his cup part way to his lips and looked pained.

"Not you, too Janet. Judson Parker's weaseled

his way into the heart of every woman in this community in order to sway votes."

Janet had no sooner opened her mouth to reply to that outrageous charge when her comments were interrupted by the arrival of Judson Parker himself. Judson had been making a circuit of the hall, slapping backs, bowing to the ladies and tickling the smaller children under the chin. He had strolled up behind the Kings and noticed where they were looking.

"Well, I must say, that's a very captivating daughter you've got there, Mrs. King."

Janet glowed with motherly pride and grew hospitable.

"My husband and I would have to agree. You will you have some punch, won't you, Mr. Parker?"

As it had been the punch bowl Judson had had his eye on in the first place, he readily accepted a glass. Announcing prizes was hot work, and the beads of perspiration had now made their way down as far as Judson's stiff, damp collar.

"Thank you very much."

As Judson gulped down the punch, which was a very colorful mix of grape and orange, Mrs. Lawson waved from the other side of the hall. Janet, dying to share her opinion of Mrs. Potts's pie, excused herself and hurried off to join her. Judson, finding himself alone with Alec, suddenly slapped a fat, ingratiating arm over Alec's shoulders. It was a bit like having an octopus drop a tentacle down from the ceiling on him without warning, and Alec had to stop himself from squirming.

"I hope you don't mind my attending this gathering, Alec," Judson said pompously. "It affords me an opportunity to get to meet some of the fine constituents in Avonlea, so I'll be better able to serve them after I'm elected."

"I was hoping you'd left your politics behind tonight, Mr. Parker," was Alec's reply.

At Alec's prickly tone, Judson choked slightly on the last of his punch. Being a politician, he recovered quickly.

"Well, I've found most people around here eager to talk to me," he answered, with just an edge of sharpness evident through his oozing affability.

Alec could no longer disguise his dislike and gave up trying.

"You're confident you're going to win, aren't you?"

This was pretty well a direct challenge. Judson set down his empty glass and puffed out his chest so expansively that the buttons holding his jacket closed nearly screamed aloud for mercy.

"A leader has to have confidence. Have you had a chance to look at some of that literature I gave your daughter to give to you?"

Alec wasn't going to get dragged into a discussion of campaign literature—not at a party, and not with a candidate who had grape punch dribbled on his chin.

"Well, we've always found our representative, David Amsberry, to be a good man."

Judson's unctuous air was beginning to falter and his smile look pasted on—which only encouraged Alec.

"We're strongly in support of him here in Avonlea," Alec plunged on obstinately, "and we're not about to change that, Mr. Parker."

The fat arm slid off Alec's shoulder, letting Alec rake in a breath of relief. Speaking his mind turned out to be so satisfying that he kept right on going, regardless of whether he was at a party or not.

"And if you were any kind of a leader, you'd come and talk to me directly instead of handing out pamphlets and trying to influence the vote with gifts, prizes and flattery."

By now, Judson was turning a purple shade

that would soon match the punch on his chin. He held on tight to the fact that he knew a few secrets Alec did not.

"You'd be surprised at the amount of support we've garnered this last week, Alec. I have felt that any man can be swayed in his thinking."

Rather pointedly, Judson darted a glance to his left. Amos Spry, who happened to be standing there, suddenly looked embarrassed. Alec saw Amos as a potential ally, and didn't notice his embarrassment.

"Well," said Alec, "I wouldn't be so sure of that, Mr. Parker. Our principles run marrow-deep— right, Amos?"

As though he had suddenly developed a nervous condition, Amos jerked his head at Alec's words but said nothing in response. Judson nodded in satisfaction. His purple shade started to recede again. He spotted Herschel in the crowd.

"Oh, Herschel," Judson called out, determined to regain the advantage. "Well, who have we decided on for the prize?"

It was pure fiction that the prize was to be given out for merit, and Herschel had been well instructed. He cleared his throat deferentially.

"Well, I thought we decided that the King girl was the most flamboyant contender."

Herschel's voice, in spite of its diffidence, carried over to Felicity. Felicity's best efforts had not cajoled Edward into finding a partner for Clemmie, so she had settled for trying to keep herself somewhere under Herschel's gaze. Now she was back beside Clemmie, and she lit up all over at Herschel's words. Even as Felicity smiled in pure elation at Clemmie, Judson turned back to Alec King.

"Well, I told you your daughter was captivating, Alec. Yeah, I guess I'm just going to have to ensure she wins."

Judson was now bent on proving that he could sway even Alec King and thought he had hit upon the price of Alec's cooperation. But if he thought he could buy Alec with a prize for best costume, he was sadly mistaken. Alec was, even then, turning away in disgust.

"You know, you and I should get to know each other better after the election's over," Judson said to Alec, stepping closer and showing every sign of slapping an arm over Alec's shoulder again.

Alec stiffened, refusing the bait once and for all.

"You're barking up the wrong tree, Mr. Parker. I'm not about to sell my vote to anyone. Neither is anyone else in Avonlea."

For both men, the pretense of friendliness was over. When Judson Parker smiled through his teeth now, it was in an openly gloating and predatory manner.

"That's where you're wrong, Mr. King. You can open any lock. All you have to do is find the right key."

With a curt nod, Judson Parker strode away. Alec, very glad to see him go, edged through the crowd to rejoin his wife. Janet had been watching the prickly exchange and frowned in puzzlement.

"What was that all about, Alec?"

All she got for answer was a grunt and a mutter. Alec did not consider the matter fit for discussion, even with his wife.

Out on the dance floor, a square dance was in progress, and Felicity was in the midst of it, showing off her costume and expecting to hear her name called out at any moment. Clemmie, left on her own again, decided there was nothing for it but to try the refreshment table. Besides, Nelly Shatford was sitting there, dressed in a bedsheet and wearing a painted wire halo for her angel costume. Gathering her resolve, Clemmie started forward. An angel seemed a fairly safe bet to practice her new social skills upon.

"Isn't it a lovely gathering?" Clemmie piped

up as soon as she got within range. "How are you this evening?"

Unfortunately, Clemmie still sounded so much like a parrot that Nelly Shatford was startled out of reaching for a fourth chocolate cookie.

"Yes, it's fine," Nelly mumbled, aiming an answer blindly at one of Clemmie's questions.

Since Felicity had promised that the conversation would roll on naturally once Clemmie sprang her opening lines, Clemmie stood gazing at Nelly expectantly. Nelly, not a great conversationalist herself, only looked increasingly uncomfortable. In fact, her gaze slid right past Clemmie's shoulder and fastened on a figure passing just behind.

"Oh, Alice, there you are," Nelly cried, leaping up in great relief from her chair. "I was afraid you'd left."

In order to escape Clemmie's fixed gaze and get to her friend, Alice made a beeline between Clemmie and the table. Her elbow bumped Clemmie's arm. The punch in Clemmie's tightly clutched glass flew up, splattered Clemmie's chin and descended in a spreading stain all down the front of the princess costume.

Nelly Shatford fled, leaving Clemmie frozen and gasping in front of the refreshment table, brushing in horror at the sopping purple mess.

Chapter Twelve

On the stage, the fiddlers were finishing off the final reel and the accordion player brought up the end of the tune with a resounding blare. The Hall was fully packed now. The doors and windows were open to let cool air flow in over the flushed revellers. They all paused as, once again, Herschel scrambled up in front of them, waving his arms to get their attention.

"Excuse me. Pardon me again, ladies and gentlemen—Judson Parker."

As fast as he'd come, Herschel dodged out of the way to leave room for his leader. Still mopping his brow, Judson mounted the steps and stood in front of the crowd. He had such an assured tilt to his stomach and such brashness in his eye that he might already have been appropriating the airs of an elected representative.

"Sorry to interrupt again, folks," he called out, not in the least bit regretful about interrupting the fun, "but, uh, we've completed the judging, and Herschel and I want to award the prize for the best costume."

Even in the midst of her disaster, Clemmie was able to think about her friend. She gave up trying to blot at the punch stain and scurried through the crowd to Felicity as inconspicuously as she could. Her fingers were so busy trying to cover the splotch that she didn't have a free hand to straight her tiara, which was now cocked permanently sideways over the Gibson Girl knot. And though strands of hair now escaped from the knot and tickled her nose, Clemmie still gazed through them in admiration at her friend Felicity.

"Your costume is the best one here," she whispered unselfishly. There wasn't the least doubt in her mind that Felicity would walk off with the prize. Oh, it would be such a treat for Felicity to go all the way to Charlottetown to hear the famous singer.

All of the children present were standing about expectantly, some with wild hope on their faces, a great many others already glancing at Felicity's elaborate creation as though her win were a fact. In Avonlea, none of the young people could sew quite as well as Felicity, and few were willing to take as many pains to make a project perfect.

Judson stood silently for a moment, savoring the breathless attention and the feeling of power it gave him. When he was in the Legislature, all these people would have to come to him, caps in hand, to ask for his favor. And the ones that were against him now, like Alec King—oh, how he would make them squirm!

"The, uh, winner for the best costume is none other than..." Judson expertly stretched out the suspense, "Jane Spry!"

A moment of blinking disbelief greeted this announcement. Jane Spry was one of the girls who couldn't be bothered much with needle-work. As Bo Peep, she wore a school dress with one of her mother's aprons tied over it. Onto this, she had tacked a droopy bow at the shoulder. On her head she wore something that looked like an old dust cap with a sprig of artificial berries dan-gling at the side. Looking at Jane, it was no wonder that Bo Peep had lost her sheep. One encounter with her and any flock of sheep would flee in the opposite direction.

Several people swiveled their heads to peer at Felicity. It was so obvious that Felicity King's cos-tume was the best one in the competition that some of the crowd imagined they had heard Judson wrong. Only when Judson began to take the envelope containing the tickets out of his pocket did the villagers suddenly remember their manners and clap politely for Jane.

As for Felicity, she was standing motionless with shock even as Jane Spry trotted ecstatically up towards the podium to snatch up her winnings. Clemmie, worried about the absolutely crushed expression creeping across Felicity's face, forgot all about her punch stain and patted Felicity on the shoulder in a vain attempt at comfort.

"Come along, little lady," Judson was saying to Jane as he reached down to help her up the steps. "Up you come. Well done, and, uh, a well-deserved prize for your efforts."

Judson hadn't actually taken a close look at Jane before his abrupt decision to grant her the prize, and he was a little taken aback. However, Jane was a Spry and her father had a vote, so Judson considered the prize well appointed. He rose to the occasion by shaking Jane's hand ceremoniously.

"I look forward to seeing you and your guest in my box in Charlottetown. Thank you very much, ladies and gentlemen, and thank you for a wonderful party."

Standing beside Judson, Jane looked more like a gift-wrapped potato than anything resembling a shepherdess. And as for enjoying Nellie Melba, everyone knew the Sprys were all tone-deaf. Jane didn't care at all. Grinning, she waved the envelope at Sally, puffed herself up with arrogance and left the podium amidst another thin spatter of applause. Judson lumbered down behind her, with the air of having done his job well. He did not realize that he had just given Avonlea a graphic demonstration of the favoritism, manipulation and unfairness that would prevail should he really become their elected representative.

Felicity, the public victim of Judson's machinations, turned in confusion to Clemmie.

"But everyone agreed that my costume was bound to win," she protested in a wounded voice.

Alec King overheard his daughter and laid a worldly-wise hand on her shoulder. The injustice of life had just struck his daughter a reeling blow, and he wanted to soften the impact.

"It wasn't a prize for best costume, Felicity," he informed her. "It was a reward for votes."

To Alec, Jane's win only meant that Judson was corrupt and Amos Spry was somehow the target of Judson's connivance. To Felicity, it meant that she hadn't won because her father had made Judson Parker angry with him. He must have decided not to vote for Mr. Parker and told the man so out loud. In doing so, he had lost her the prize.

"He said I'd win!" she fired back in outrage. "You and your principles. It's all your fault!"

Leaving her father with his eyebrows shooting skyward in surprise, Felicity whipped her shimmery train around and stormed out of the room.

Chapter Thirteen

Felicity fled into the vestibule, plopped down on a wooden bench in the corner and sat hunched in disappointment and fury. Who knows how long she might have stayed like that had Clemmie not followed her out and timidly approached the bench.

"I'm sorry you didn't win, Felicity," Clemmie said in commiseration. "It wasn't fair."

That was pretty obvious. Felicity let out an injured sigh and gathered her skirts around her.

"Oh, I don't care, Clemmie. I just want to go home."

"So do I," Clemmie agreed. It had been no fun for her either, standing around stained with punch and having even angels flee from her attempts at conversation. "I'll go get our coats."

Clemmie hurried into the cloakroom only to find her brother lounging next to the coatrack. He was swinging one heel idly the way he did when he had some kind of plan in mind.

"I'm here to get Felicity's coat," Clemmie told him by way of explanation. Warily, she tried to squeeze by him. Edward was still looking as fierce as a pirate, and there was no telling what sort of mischief he was capable of, even to little sisters.

In an instant, Edward had Felicity's coat in his own hands and was holding it out of Clemmie's reach. He'd probably been waiting for this moment.

"I'll take it to her," Edward said even as Clemmie tried to get hold of the garment.

"She asked me to take it to her," Clemmie protested, but she was no match for Edward. He waved the coat above his head like a trophy and started for the cloakroom door. Clemmie had no choice but to pick up her own coat and follow him.

Outside, in the vestibule, Felicity was not to escape without the final reckoning. As was inevitable, Sally Potts and Jane Spry had hunted her down and descended upon the bench.

"Well, Felicity," Sally gloated, "hand it over."

She stuck her fat palm practically in Felicity's face.

"Hand what over?" Felicity asked, trying to drag her mind back from the loss of the costume prize.

"Your tiara, of course."

"You lost the bet," Jane jeered. "Clemmie wasn't at all popular, and you know it."

Sally Potts was exalting so much over besting Felicity King that it was a wonder her feet remained on the ground.

"I told you you couldn't make a silk purse out of a sow's ear," she crowed.

Edward, with a still-indignant Clemmie on his heels, had skidded to a halt just inside the cloakroom door. Disbelief slowly spread across his face as he hovered there, Felicity's coat flung over his arm, listening.

"You had as much chance of winning this bet as you would have of kissing a frog and having him turn into a handsome Prince!" Sally needled, completely oblivious of the audience around the corner.

With one hand, Jane Spry waved her envelope with the prize tickets in front of Felicity's nose, and the other stuck out to claim the tiara.

"Hand it over. You and Clemmie will only ever be the losers we said you were."

All the stinging retorts Felicity might have made had quite fled her mind. After all, Clemmie was covered with punch and Jane had the costume prize. There seemed nothing for it but to concede defeat. Slowly, wearily, Felicity reached up and began to take off her tiara.

The instant it was free of Felicity's hair, Sally

snatched it away and slapped it onto her own head. The tiara sat sparkling there, so much at odds with Sally's unpleasant face and tablecloth cloak as to suggest that Red Riding Hood had turned to crime and taken up burglary on the side.

"I guess *I'm* the princess this year after all."

Chortling to each other, Sally and Jane ran off to examine their booty. Clemmie and Edward looked at each other, still frozen where they stood. Clemmie was just beginning to realize the sort of trick that had been played on her. Her young face crumpled with misery at Felicity's betrayal. Edward the pirate now scowled in grim understanding, all hint of his previous high spirits gone. Though he often teased or ignored Clemmie, he was still her brother when it came to the serious matters. And Edward had just suffered a rather serious disillusionment about a girl he had once admired. He stalked into the vestibule, forbidding as Captain Kidd, and flung Felicity's coat into her lap.

"Come on, Clemmie," he rasped out. "Don't waste your time with her."

To make sure she came, Edward grasped Clemmie by the arm and hauled her after him towards the outside door. Clemmie was too overcome with dismay to resist.

"I thought you were my friend," she flung over her shoulder at Felicity as she and Edward disappeared from sight.

In horror, Felicity realized that she must have been overheard, that Clemmie knew all about the bet with Sally Potts. She had told herself that she only wanted to help Clemmie. Now, looking over the ruin of the evening, she saw that her efforts to remake Clemmie and win Sally's locket had only botched everything.

After a moment, she picked up her coat from where Edward had thrown it and pulled it over her now forlorn princess costume. As she did so, Judson Parker, attended by Herschel, came through the vestibule looking supremely self-satisfied. Absorbed in conversation, neither noticed the withering glance Felicity threw at them as she stood up and left.

In the cloakroom, Herschel and Judson shrugged into their own coats. Both were pleased with the night's events.

"I think we've got this backwater all sewn up, don't you?"

Herschel ventured. Judson paused, not so sure.

"Well, David Amsberry seems to have a smattering of support here still."

"I hear he's coming to Avonlea to campaign tomorrow," Herschel said.

Part of Herschel's job was to keep close tabs on what the opposition was up to. Judson was surprised and became obviously uneasy.

"That so? Perhaps I need to show him just how much support I have here in Avonlea."

"Why? You've already got everyone in your back pocket." Herschel hadn't been present at the peppery exchange with Alec King.

"Maybe I have to show him who's boss," Judson muttered as he and Herschel left the Avonlea Town Hall.

Felicity had a glum journey home and, since her conscience proved a thorny bedfellow, a very uncomfortable night. As the consequences of her actions became more and more painfully clear, Felicity just had to seek relief by talking them over with a friend—even if that friend had already vowed to have nothing to do with her.

The next day found her at Rose Cottage, pacing back and forth in the parlor distractedly. Sara Stanley was sitting primly in the middle of the huge old sofa, listening to Felicity's outpourings. She had to keep her lips pressed together very tight in order to prevent herself from saying "I told you so!"

"Oh, Sara," Felicity was lamenting, "you were so right. Why didn't I listen? I never thought there could be anything worse than losing my prize. Now," Felicity measured the depth of the catastrophe, "even Edward won't talk to me. I never thought I'd see the day when I would complain about that. But now I *do* care."

"You were pretty mean to Clemmie," Sara allowed, folding her hands in front of her.

"I thought that I was helping her. She did want to become more popular."

Sara looked even more severe. "I warned you that it was bound to hurt her feelings if she found out. Why you were so taken by Sally Potts and Jane Spry is beyond me. You don't even like them."

Felicity flung an arm out in bafflement. "I don't know."

She only knew that Sally and Jane had such a way of goading a person that you could end up agreeing to any sort of craziness to shut them up.

After a moment, Felicity came and sat down beside Sara, her face brooding.

"I just can't stand the thought of everyone disliking me. I like to have lots of friends."

To Sara, this was a poor explanation for commerce with the two school troublemakers.

"Lots of friends who would just as soon cut you to pieces as look at you?" Sara flared. "Anyway, Clemmie and I are still your friends."

Felicity didn't believe this. She remembered the wounded look on Clemmie's face as Clemmie had stumbled out of the Town Hall.

"Clemmie will probably never speak to me again, Sara. How did you know this was going to happen?"

Felicity seemed to be expecting Sara to confess she had clairvoyant powers. Sara had merely paid attention to the facts.

"Well, as Aunt Hetty always says, if you do something wrong, it's bound to come back at you somehow. Now, what you have to do is ask Clemmie to forgive you."

"I know," Felicity replied, sighing deeply. Getting Clemmie to forgive her was going to be no easy task.

Chapter Fourteen

Judson Parker must have been worried indeed about the dangers of David Amsberry's impending visit. He took action swiftly, furtively and in the dark of night. When the Avonlea people woke up on the morning Mr. Amsberry was slated to come, they discovered the village itself and all the farms around plastered top to bottom with Judson Parker campaign posters. Judson leered at them from stakes on lawns, from garden fences, the sides of rain barrels and the walls of every single building on the street. It was as if Avonlea had been invaded overnight and occupied by an invading army of paper Parkers, all smiling identically about the feat. One way or another, Judson seemed determined to grab possession of Avonlea.

Mrs. Biggins, who ran the boarding house next to the general store, marched out onto her lawn and surveyed the house. Two posters had gone up before dawn without her hearing a thing.

"How dare that dreadful man put signs on my porch?"

Angrily, Mrs. Biggins ripped down the offending posters and flung them into the trash.

The King buggy rattled down the street, passing Edward and Clemmie Ray, who had just picked up some sugar for their mother. As the buggy slowly rolled to a halt in front of the general store, Felicity jumped down from beside her father and ran after them. She was trying her best not to sound wildly anxious.

"Hello, Clemmie. Hello, Edward," she called out, hoping that she could act as though nothing had happened at the Harvest Party.

Her hope was in vain. Without a word, Edward and Clemmie continued walking. Their heads were in the air, their eyes straight ahead, as though they hadn't even heard Felicity. This shocking change from their usual behavior brought it home to Felicity just how offended they still must be with her. Holding onto her hat, Felicity raced after them.

"Clemmie, wait. I really need to talk to you. Please, let me explain."

Clemmie turned her face away and walked even faster. Her cheeks were pale and smudges under her eyes hinted that perhaps she hadn't been sleeping so well either. Edward grew impatient with her short strides and tugged at her arm.

"Come on, Clemmie, let's go."

Clemmie opened her mouth as if to say something, but Edward had already thrust himself between her and Felicity, holding the bag of sugar like a shield.

"And you can just leave my sister alone, Felicity King," he warned fearsomely, without a trace of the teasing usually in his voice when speaking to Felicity.

In sheer dismay, Felicity stopped in her tracks, watching helplessly as the two stiff backs disappeared around a corner. The awful scope of the disaster began to open up before her eyes. What if Clemmie and Edward never spoke to her again?

Sighing, Felicity turned back towards the general store where a number of people were rapidly gathering. Harmon Andrews, Alec King, Amos Spry, Mrs. Potts and Mrs. Lawson were all standing on the steps, furious about Judson's signs.

"When I think of all the work I did on the front garden, clearing my sightlines," Harmon complained, "grading, seeding...and now all you can see is Judson Parker's face."

Harmon held up a half-torn Parker poster he had pulled down from his fence. Judson's portrait didn't seem to strike Harmon's fancy as scenery, for he crumpled it up in disgust.

"He's defaced the whole town is what he's done," Mrs. Lawson sputtered. Having a business right in the heart of Avonlea, Mrs. Lawson was doubly sensitive about how the neighborhood looked. Anyone coming to town now would think the whole place bought, paid for and practically gift-wrapped by the man.

Mrs. Potts, though dressed in a striped purple coat and sporting a hat bristling all over with artificial cherries, suddenly found she, too, had developed a sense of taste. Or rather, she had gauged the mood of the village and prudently changed sides.

"And after all the Avonlea Improvement Society did to beautify it," she exclaimed. "It's not right." If this was Parker's idea of decorating Avonlea before the election, goodness knows what he would do afterward.

"You should never have let him donate that prize to the Harvest Party," Mrs. Lawson said. "Now he's going to think that we owe him something."

All the cherries on Mrs. Potts's hat rattled self-righteously. She developed a pained, martyred look.

"Well, Elvira May I'll admit that he tried to get round me with flattery and promises. But he has no public spirit, that man."

Harmon took another twist at the already demolished poster he had brought in.

"Think's he's got the whole town sewn up, does he?"

Mrs. Potts sniffed at the very idea. Truth was not her strong point. Backing the winning side was. In that, her daughter Sally had come by her ability to connive quite honestly.

"He's a born manipulator, all right. I saw through him from the start, didn't I, Elvira May?"

Mrs. Lawson was far too clever to get herself embroiled in that question—especially since she remembered the scenes from her store window when Judson had first come to Avonlea. She took another tack altogether.

"David Amsberry would never stoop to something like this. He has too much regard for public opinion."

"Guess you were right about him all along, Alec," Amos Spry said to Alec King, who had been leaning against the door jamb and listening in satisfaction to the conversation. "Seems a lot of us were carried away by foolish promises."

Amos Spry could tell the difference between an elegant princess and a floppy-looking Bo Peep, even if that Bo Peep happened to be his own daughter. It was the very fact that Jane had won the prize that had changed Amos's mind about having anything to do with Judson Parker. If Judson were capable of twisting a kid's costume contest around for his own purposes, who knew what the man would do when he got the power that came with lending out money. Why, Parker might get up on the wrong side of the bed one day and decide to foreclose on the Sprys. No, far better to take one's chances with the bank. At least there a fellow knew where he stood, even if it meant taking more of his money troubles to the manager in Summerside.

"Well," announced Harmon Andrews with a hitch at his overalls, "I'll tell you one thing for sure. Judson Parker's not getting my vote."

"Nor mine!" Amos Spry decided there had to be lots more ways to cook potatoes that winter.

"Nor my husband's," said Mrs. Lawson, glancing over her shoulder at the unsuspecting man working away inside the store.

Apparently, second thoughts about the events of the last few days were hitting quite a number of people in Avonlea. David Amsberry arrived on schedule and gave such a reasonable, reassuring speech that all who heard it wondered what on earth anyone had ever seen in Judson Parker.

A very sober Felicity was one of the listeners. She drove home in silence beside her father and remained silent until supper time when it was her turn to set the table. The kitchen table, of course, invoked recent and troubling memories about bad bargains struck there.

Behind Felicity, Alec sat in a chair polishing his boots. Relations had been strained between father and daughter ever since Felicity's furious words of the night before. Now she wanted very much to put things right, but didn't quite know how to do it.

Alec, pretending to be busy with his boots, watched Felicity's inner struggle as she walked about laying down the plates. Something like a knowing smile tugged at one corner of his mouth, but he said nothing to prompt his daughter; she had got herself into this. She would have to get herself out.

Before she got to the forks and spoons, Felicity screwed up her courage.

"Father," she began, "there's something that I have to tell you."

Alec put the top back on the boot polish.

"Yes, what's that?"

Felicity hesitated, biting her lip.

"I was really angry with you at the Harvest Party because I thought that it was your fault that I lost the prize. But I want you to know that I don't feel that way any more."

All of a sudden, Alec was smiling and setting his boots aside.

"Well, princess, it's not always easy to do but," he stood up with a stretch and walked over to his daughter, "I figure you can't get everyone to agree with you all the time about everything, so...might as well just do what you think is right in the first place."

This piece of advice, given a week earlier, might have saved Felicity much tribulation. But then again, it might not, for it was the sort of thing a girl usually had to learn the hard way.

Felicity looked up earnestly at her father.

"I realize that now, and I'm really proud of you."

Felicity's words were worth more than pure gold to her father, but he didn't quite have time to say so, since Felix and Cecily were clattering in through the door for their supper. Instead, Alec leaned over and gave Felicity a smacking kiss of approval on the forehead. Nothing more was needed. From Felicity's smile, her father's message had got through loud and clear.

Chapter Fifteen

To lose a friend was a dreadful feeling. Felicity had had no idea how dreadful until she discovered that Clemmie really wanted nothing to do with her. She hardly slept the night after Clemmie marched away from her on the street. Could it have been only the previous Friday, Felicity thought, that she had been standing in front of the entire school congratulating herself for having so many friends?

School, in fact, was to be Felicity's next ordeal. The first morning back after the Harvest Party was a difficult one. Jane Spry and Sally Potts snickered together and looked insufferably smug. Clemmie kept her head down whenever Felicity looked her way, and even Cecily was afraid to talk to Clemmie, in case her anger at Felicity extended to the whole King family, including her. Edward expressed not the faintest interest in tweaking Felicity's hair, passing her notes or even taking revenge with his trusty rubber bands. Hetty sprang a surprise spelling test, then announced that she expected to get through a good number of the "Harvest Time" recitations that day.

By the time recess rolled around, tensions were high. The children exploded from their desks and dashed for the relief afforded by fifteen minutes of yelling and running about outside. Felicity got up more slowly and walked over to Sara. Sara seemed to be the only friend Felicity had left in the world.

"Clemmie's going to give her speech after

recess," Felicity said gloomily. She would have to endure the torture of seeing Clemmie look everywhere but in her direction. Or maybe Clemmie's confidence had been so shattered by her experiences at the Harvest Party that she wouldn't be able to give a speech at all.

For lack of anything else to do, Felicity and Sara drifted to the cloakroom to get their coats. But if Felicity was downhearted, Sara still had some spirit left. She spotted Clemmie going out of the school behind the others and gave Felicity a bolstering prod in the ribs.

"Come on, Felicity, try talking to her again."

Felicity hesitated, afraid of another icy rejection. However, things couldn't be any worse than they were at the moment, so she might as well make another effort. She would gladly give a dozen tiaras just to have Clemmie smile at her again. Just as Clemmie got to the door, Felicity ran after her and caught her by the arm. Tactfully, Sara hung back in the cloakroom.

Clemmie gave a start at Felicity's touch, but didn't shake her off. Surprised, Felicity got between Clemmie and the door. Who knew when she'd get another opportunity like this to explain herself?

"Clemmie," Felicity began in a rush, "you

have every reason to be angry at me, but I never meant to hurt you. And if it's worth anything at all to you, then...I really like you, Clemmie. I always have. And I like you because of who you are, not because of who you could be. You're sincere and you're loyal. I was wrong. I—I took advantage of you, and I am sorry."

Clemmie had stood with her head down through the entire speech, looking very much like a little cat hunched in the rain. Now, Felicity held her breath in apprehension about how Clemmie was going to respond.

For a good, long moment, Clemmie didn't move at all. Then, to Felicity's complete astonishment, Clemmie's round, earnest face came up and regarded Felicity gravely. She seemed to have been waiting for just such an opening. And she couldn't possibly have mistaken the sincerity in Felicity's heartfelt words.

"I was very nervous at the Harvest Party," Clemmie conceded. "But I know you were only trying to help me. We're still friends, Felicity."

No condemned person who had just had a terrible sentence lifted from her head could have felt happier than Felicity. She let out a squeal and grabbed Clemmie in a joyful hug.

Sara laughed, too, to see the two friends

united again. In infinite relief, the three ran out to the schoolyard and caught up with Cecily, bursting to talk over everything between them. So little time had passed, yet they each had a hundred things to tell the others.

After recess, the time for Clemmie's speech quickly arrived. Head held high, Clemmie rose from her desk and repeated her journey of the previous week to the front of the room. Though the terrifying words "Harvest Time" were chalked on the blackboard behind her, Clemmie bore their proximity with surprising fortitude. She clasped her hands demurely in front of her and cleared her throat. Everyone waited anxiously—except Jane Spry and Sally Potts. Incorrigible, they started to snicker, fully expecting to bedevil Clemmie into flight once again.

Hetty, positioned at the back, suddenly thumped on the desk next to Sally, making her jump in her seat.

"Now that the party is finally over, I expect absolute attention, do you hear? So does Clemmie. You may begin, Clemmie."

With Jane and Sally temporarily quelled. Clemmie had a chance to start without harassment. Also, after having been through the fires of the Harvest Party, Clemmie now found public speaking in front of her classmates much less hair-raising than she had previously imagined. Besides, this time her mind wasn't an echoing, panicky blank. This time, Clemmie had something to say.

"Harvest Time," she began bravely. "This year Harvest Time was not what I expected. I'm not certain of how to say this...because I'm not very good at expressing myself. But I feel I have to say it."

No one had expected this kind of theme from Clemmie. Restless bodies settled down. Hetty took an empty seat and listened more intently— as did the rest of the class.

"Sometimes people will laugh at you, and not everyone is going to like you. But the most important thing in life is to be yourself."

Clemmie paused and looked straight at Sally Potts and Jane Spry. Sally got ready to make a face and Jane toyed with her slate. Seeing Clemmie's unwavering eye, they both thought the better of trying to torment her. In fact, if they persisted, they felt they ran the danger of being mentioned by name in Clemmie's speech.

As for Felicity, she was smiling now. What Clemmie had just said sounded very familiar. It was what Felicity's own father had told her just the evening before.

Clemmie looked back at Felicity, Sara and Cecily and drew silent support from her friends. Even Edward, just behind Felicity, was looking pleased with his sister and feeling benevolent towards Felicity. Edward had seen Clemmie, Felicity, Cecily and Sara talking a mile a minute at recess, and knew the feud between the Rays and the Kings had come to an end.

"That's the only way you can have the confidence in yourself to know what is right and what is wrong," Clemmie went on. "Harvest Time is still my most favorite time of year, but this year for a different reason. That's all."

A philosophical silence filled the classroom for some moments after Clemmie had finished. Even Hetty hesitated, obviously moved by the thoughts Clemmie expressed. It really was amazing, she thought, what a well-chosen recitation topic could do for a child.

"Thank you, Clemmie," Hetty said at last. "Ah, take your seat."

Having finally overcome her fear of public speaking, Clemmie sat down, looking as proud as though she had just conquered a dragon. Hetty walked to the front of the room, caught herself gazing thoughtfully out the window and jerked herself back to the business at hand.

"Well...yes, class, uh, open your spellers and, uh, turn to the verb section at the end."

The restoration of good fellowship seemed to make the rest of the school day rush by in a minute. Before anyone knew what was happening, Felicity, Cecily, Sara and Clemmie found themselves in the cloakroom getting ready to go home. Felicity was bubbling over with cordiality and didn't want the companionship to end.

"Clemmie, why don't you come over to my house," Felicity invited impulsively, "and help Sara and me with our tobacco quilts that we're working on for the winter bazaar?"

What a signal honor! Felicity never let anyone else touch her carefully planned quilt. Clemmie glowed happily, feeling important all over again to have Felicity and Sara paying so much attention to her.

"All right."

Felicity laughed and gave her tam a pat.

"Oh, good! And I promise I won't fix your hair or...make you straighten your shoulders or straighten your walk." She had decided that Clemmie was just fine exactly the way she was.

"I've sort of been practicing it anyhow,"

Clemmie acknowledged. She wasn't about to pass up such useful tips on social advancement, just because they had got her into a spot of bother at the Harvest Party.

Edward stomped into the cloakroom from outside. His cheeks were already red and he wound his scarf more tightly around his neck.

"Clemmie, are you coming? I'm freezing."

Felicity hesitated only a moment, even though she had suffered twice from Edward's elastic band that afternoon.

"Um..." Clemmie is coming over to my house. Would you like to come?"

Edward had never really stopped liking Felicity. Now the wicked glint was back in his eyes as he pretended to ponder the invitation.

"Well, only if you promise not to make me walk with a book on my head, or straighten my shoulders."

"What?"

Felicity's astonishment made Edward slap his thighs.

"Well, I saw the whole lesson through your window," he crowed, dodging back out of Felicity's reach just in case.

"Edward!" Felicity and Clemmie cried simultaneously.

Edward turned and ran out of the cloakroom with the girls in hot pursuit.

Outside, there had already been a light dusting of snow. All the children were shouting and throwing handfuls of the cold white stuff at each other as they streamed out of the schoolyard. Shouting happily, Edward, Felicity, Cecily, Clemmie and Sara ran off together with the rest. For the five of them, it was indeed harvest time. Their harvest was an overflowing measure of friendship.

❧   ❧   ❧

Timeless Classics The Whole Family Will Enjoy By
L. M. Montgomery